LION ON THE JOB

PARANORMAL DATING AGENCY

NEW YORK TIMES and USA TODAY
BESTSELLING AUTHOR

MILLY TAIDEN

Published By

Latin Goddess Press

Winter Springs, FL 32708

http://millytaiden.com

Lion on the Job

Copyright © 2019 by Milly Taiden

Edited by: Tina Winograd

Cover: Willsin Rowe

Lion on the Job

Remy Leandros is busting his fur to make the Lakeside Pride stronger than ever. It's as easy as one, two, three. Or so he thought. He's afraid if something doesn't change soon, their numbers may decrease. What he doesn't count on is his mate coming to his rescue. Wait. Mate? He doesn't want a sexy, sensual, smart mate staying in his guest room. Much less saving his ass.

Genevieve Monroe's stage play stars lion shifters. What better way to learn about these big felines than from real shifters? With help from Gerri Wilder, she and her crew are staying a couple weeks with the pride. And Gen herself is about to get up close and real personal with the big, sexy alpha of the pride. An alpha so hot, she wants to strip naked and purr like a cat in heat.

As a producer, Gen's used to drama, but the performance playing out in the pride is beyond her expertise, especially when she's personally threatened. Remy tries to protect his mate, but she's determined to do what she wants, how she wants. But when she goes missing, it's up to Remy to find her before the curtain closes.

— For my readers.

Your support means the world to me.

ONE

"Remy Leandros, you hardheaded pussycat, come inside already. Stop pacing and open the damn door." Gerri sat at her kitchen table with a smirk on her face and a cup of tea in her hand.

The door finally opened and Remy, lion alpha of the Lakeside Pride, scowled at her. "Why do you keep sending Bertha to me with invites for tea? I told you now is not a good time for a mate. My pride is still hurting after Megan's betrayal, and bringing in someone new isn't a good idea."

Gerri shook her head at Remy and gestured to the chair across from her. When lioness Megan, a member of the Lakeside Pride, one of

Remy's own, had caused chaos and tried to destroy the peace between the lions and the wolves of the area, it nearly killed his pride's morale. Now, it was up to Remy to help piece that back together and Gerri had some ideas on how to make it happen. "Please sit. I respect your wishes. That's not why I asked you to come see me." Gerri picked up her tea and took a sip, watching Remy over the rim. "Would you like a cup of tea?"

"No, thank you. What I would like, is for you to spit it out. Why do you want to talk to me?"

She set the cup on the saucer in front of her and sighed, cocking her head. "Bertha is concerned with the pack's morale. They are down in the dumps, as she likes to say. We thought we could have an event of some kind. One that would bring mates to your pride and provide some levity. You all suffered quite the disloyalty." Gerri leaned back in her chair. She waited while Remy scowled at her. She counted in her head. It took him three seconds before he was out of his chair and pacing her dining room. Poor kitten. He needed someone to help him handle his pride and she planned on giving him just that. A partner.

"Okay, if I agree to this crazy idea, what do you have in mind?" Remy walked back to the table and dropped into the chair with a loud sigh.

"A friend of a friend is in a theater group, and they are looking to study a lion pride for a week or two. They want to do their play justice. So someone thought seeing real lions up close and safely was the best way.

"They came to me for help. I mentioned it to Bertha who, of course, jumped on the idea and emailed you to meet with me to discuss it."

Remy frowned at Gerri, his face scrunched up as he thought about what she said. The lion was tough and sweet, but could be so damn difficult at times. He sat down with a huff. "How do you know my pride has any mates in that troupe? You haven't met them yet."

Gerri rolled her eyes, holding back a smirk. "A lady never tells her secrets. Do you have room for the director and some of the actors to join you in your area of the woods?"

Remy's chair squeaked as he shifted uncomfortably. "I assume this is one of those requests I simply can't refuse."

"You could refuse, but why would you want to keep your pride from finding their mates? Sounds a bit selfish to me." Gerri shrugged, stood and walked to the door. "How many people can you accommodate?"

Remy chuckled and got up from his seat.

Gerri grinned at herself. Too easy.

"Two can stay with me, and there are two empty cabins. We can provide beds for at least eight. More if they want to share beds. I'll tell the pride to expect them and get the places cleaned up."

She nodded and opened the door. "Bertha is handling that. I'll let you know when they're coming." She turned to face him with arched brows. "And, Remy, be nice to them, please."

Gerri smiled sweetly at Remy as he walked through the door with a quiet snarl of indignation. She shut the door and headed into her office to call Bertha and let her know the plan worked. She picked up the phone and waited patiently for Bertha to answer.

"So?"

Gerri laughed, delighted that Bertha was in on things. "Hello, dear, I do love how you answer the phone."

Bertha snorted and Gerri could picture her face clearly. She would be scowling but not really meaning it. She didn't have the patience for the niceties that society deemed necessary. "Tell me how he took the news."

Gerri paused while she waited for Bertha to stop issuing orders to someone on her side of the phone. "Resigned is the best way to describe his reaction. Now, how are you going to make sure she is in his spare bedroom, hmmm?"

Bertha cackled. For an elderly shifter, she was quite spunky. "That's the easy part. I'll tell him I am handling everything, and he won't say no. He finds it easier to let me do what I want rather than fight me."

"You mean you act typical southern crazy old woman and he's too afraid to rile you up and lets you get away with it. One day, Bertha, he will see through your act." Gerri wouldn't change Bertha for the world, but she did love to rile up Remy.

"I will just promise to wear pants to the next pride meeting, and he will let me do whatever I want."

Gerri choked on a laugh. "You didn't!"

Bertha grumbled, "Of course, I did. He wouldn't let me redecorate his cabin!"

"Did it work?"

Bertha chuckled. "No, he still wouldn't let me decorate, but he knows I am serious now."

Gerri shook her head and tried not to laugh. She really didn't want to encourage Bertha's outlandish ways. "Should I warn the theater people about you?"

"Nah, they are dramatic enough. I will fit right in. I have to go. Gerri? Thank you for your help." Bertha hung up quickly and Gerri set the phone down. One more call to make and things should be moving right along.

Remy wouldn't resist once he met his mate, and if anyone else happened to find theirs at the same time... Well, nothing wrong with that at all.

TWO

Genevieve sat at her desk in the back of the theater and stared at her computer screen. The play was in two months and she had to fill the leading lady spot. Having the actress back out last minute added a ton of stress on her shoulders. Thankfully, Gerri Wilder was recommended to her. Studying a lion pride up close and personal was exactly what the troupe needed. One less thing to stress about at least.

A knock at the door had her looking up. "Hey, Gen, we have three actresses waiting to read for the part. Are you ready for them?"

Gen rubbed her forehead and pushed her chair back. "Let's get this over with, please. The sooner we fill this part, the faster everything will come together." She walked around the desk and followed the assistant director, Doreen, to the stage where the woman waited.

"Thank you for coming today. Before we begin, I am going to look over your resumes. Please read through the character summary we have for you and decide if this is a part you are still interested in."

She walked down the stage steps and sat in the back row where she was hidden in the dim house lighting. The assistant director took the seat next to her. "Have you seen Bailey anywhere? I thought she wanted to be here when we auditioned the actresses."

Gen absently looked around and then back at the papers in her hand. "She may have decided she needed to learn the part better if she wanted a shot at it. Either way, she will be the understudy."

"By the way, Gerri Wilder called, and we are all set for the crew to stay with the pride as long as you think they need to. The alpha has two rooms available. I told Gerri you were coming so I think you should stay at his place. It would be a good chance to find out how the pride works."

Gen nodded absently and shuffled the papers.

"Okay, ladies, as you all are still here, we assume you have no issues with shifters or portraying them in this play, correct?" When the actresses nodded, she continued speaking.

"The leads will be staying on pride land for a bit to interact, learn from, and chat with lions. If you aren't comfortable with this, leave now." Gen watched the women shuffle their feet until one stepped forward and walked off stage.

"Okay, Wanda, you can start, please. Then you, Leslie, will be next. You may wait offstage, and my assistant will be over shortly with the name of the new leading lady." Gen leaned back in her chair and waited for the first actress to start her audition.

The woman hollered, "I'm doing a re-enactment of the restaurant scene in *When Harry Met Sally.*"

Gen's brows pulled down. It'd been a while since she'd seen that movie. She didn't immediately remember any restaurant scene. When the actress starting moaning, Gen realized what scene it was.

Oh my god, she whispered to herself. "Is she serious?"

The woman's head rolled back, a lustful groan echoing in the empty chamber. Gens face erupted into fire. Doreen smashed her hands over her mouth, quieting her laughing. The actress's breathing came in short, quick pants, her large breasts bouncing. Maybe the chick thought this was a foot-up if auditioning for male directors, but it did nothing for her. Except embarrass her more.

The woman's hands slid over her breast,

down over her stomach. Her hips swayed slightly. A loud "Oh yes" made Gen search the room for anyone else and slide down in her auditorium seat. This was a community theater, for god's sake, not the Adult Movie Channel.

On stage, the lady fell to the floor on her back, legs spread. Her ass lifted off the ground, pumping in the air, repeats of *oh god* filling the small space.

From the corner of her eye, Gen saw someone standing in the doorway. One of the young male stagehands stood gawking and gaping. "Hadley." She snapped her fingers when he didn't respond to her from only a few feet away. "Hadley," she said louder. His head whipped around to her. "Close the door."

He stepped inside and started to close the door.

She pointed at him, narrowing her eyes. "You on the other side." He ducked his head as if apologizing and scooted outside, shutting the door. Then Gen realized the place was silent. She dropped her pen and clapped. Doreen joined her.

"Thank you," Gen called out as the woman stood on the stage apron. "Great job. Next!" She bent over to search for her dropped pen. If the following audition was any worse, she'd not need to take notes. Bailey might yet have a shot at the lead.

When she looked up, a petite but pretty

young lady stood looking out with her hand shading her eyes. Gen glanced at the resumes in her hand.

"Are you Leslie?" she asked.

"Yes, ma'am. Thank you for letting me audition for you."

So far so good. "What are you doing?" Gen really hoped she wouldn't say the female version of the Harry Potter actor's nude stroll across stage in *Equus*.

"I'm going to sing the main song to *Lion King*."

Gen reconsidered her thought of nudity. "This isn't a musical," Gen said.

"Oh," Leslie frowned. "It's about lions, right?"

"Yes," Gen answered, "but there's no singing."

Leslie studied her feet for a moment. "I could just *say* the words to the song."

"Please, do." Gen shook her head, glad those on stage couldn't see her.

The actress began, lifting an arm. "From the day we arrive on the planet..."

Gens brows lifted. The girl's sound was great. Her stage voice resonated with a slight rasp that added a natural roughness. Movements were graceful and eye contact was great.

Gen leaned over to her assistant. "Tell Ms. Orgasm thanks for coming but not in this lifetime."

Doreen stared at her.

"What?" Gen said.

"You really want me to thank her for *coming*?"

Gen slapped a hand over her mouth. *Oh, god.* Had she really said that?

Doreen said, "I can tell her she was the climax of our auditions."

She tried to keep her laughing quiet. "She's at the peak of her abilities." They both giggled then Gen shooed the girl away to deal with the sticky situation.

Gen stood and came down the aisle. "Leslie, thank you." The actress stopped mid-word. "Great job. You've got the part."

The woman squealed and jumped. "Thank you so much."

"First thing we're doing is spending time with a real shifter lion pride. Be here eight a.m. Wednesday and we'll go together." She pointed stage right. "Doreen will answer any questions. See you then."

As she walked out, she turned her phone back on. During auditions, she always turned it off to not disturb the actors or mess with her focus. A notification for a voice message flashed on the screen.

She pressed keys to get to her voicemail, then accidentally hit the delete button instead of the play. "Goddammit." Oh, well. If it was important, they would call again.

THREE

Two days later, Gen walked into the theater to see the crew ready and waiting on her. She'd love a nap or a big cup of coffee right about now. Her life was constant craziness with this play, and she was exhausted. "Sorry, guys, didn't think I was running that far behind. Everyone here? Do you all want to carpool to the location? I can take three of you in my car and Bailey has a van that will hold the rest of you."

Gen didn't wait to see who would ride with her. She just turned and walked outside and climbed back in her car. A few minutes later, everyone was loaded up and they were on their way.

"Are you guys ready for this?" Gen gulped.

Good god. A real freaking Pride. Was she insane to bring humans out to hang out with shifters? "I'm kinda nervous." Gen glanced in her rearview mirror at Shelby. The woman was timid and shy until she got on stage. The transformation amazed Gen every time.

Next to her sat Ethan, who nodded with a laugh. "We are going to be staying with predators. Of course, I'm nervous!"

Gen smiled at their comments and listened to them chat for a few minutes. Next to her in the passenger seat sat Jerome. He flirted with her a lot, but she didn't think he was actually interested.

He was quieter than normal. Hopefully he wasn't getting second thoughts. He was the perfect actor for the lead, and she didn't want to have to replace him, too.

Gen was lost in thought and didn't realize how much time had passed when her GPS announced their destination was on the right in half a mile. She slowed and looked for a place to turn in. Before they found a road or even a dirt path, they spotted an older woman standing on the side of the road. She had her hands on her hips and a scowl on her face.

Gen pulled up next to her and rolled the window down. "Ma'am, are you okay? Do you need help?"

The woman barked a laugh and leaned into the car. "I'm just peachy. Tired of waiting on you all to arrive. What are you waiting on, hmm? Pull your car in and park. We have people to do and places to see." The woman turned and walked along a dirt lane away from them.

"Isn't the saying *people to see and places to go*?" Shelby glanced at everyone in the car to gauge their reactions to the odd woman.

Gen sighed. "Yes, that is the saying. If she is our contact, this could be a very, very interesting trip." Gen smiled to herself and parked the car next to the scowling lady. Everyone climbed out and grabbed their bags and stood clumped together in front of the strange woman.

"My name is Bertha. I have two cabins made up for you to stay in. We thought there were more of you, so you can split up into girls' and boys' cabins. Who's in charge here?"

Gen stepped forward "That would be me. I'm the director. My name is Genevieve Monroe, but everyone calls me Gen." Gen tried not to fidget as Bertha looked at her from head to toe.

"You'll do."

Okay then. What the hell did that mean? Gen glanced at her friends standing behind her, not quite sure what to make of her words. When she turned back, two others stood behind Bertha.

"Star, here, will escort you ladies to your

cabin. Feel free to wander around and chat with anyone. We won't bite unless you ask us nicely." Bertha smiled and Gen took a step back. "Not you, boss lady. You wait with me. Gentlemen, this is Augustus. He will show you to your cabin."

When everyone started moving away, Bertha yelled out, "Star, Augustus, make sure you bring them to the center for potluck tonight. I went hunting so we are having dee—I mean, venison."

Gen saw a couple of her crew make gagging faces. Hopefully they had normal food. She wasn't sure she could convince the crew to stay otherwise. Fuck.

She should've packed snacks. Why hadn't she thought of that until now? Shit, she might need a bag of chips if the food didn't live up to their hopes.

When she turned back to Bertha to thank her, she found she'd moved closer and stood right in front of her.

"I'll take you to Remy's cabin. He's got a place for you, and I know you will be happy there."

Bertha turned and walked away. Gen was a bit nervous about following the strange woman. Who knew what awaited her in Remy's cabin?

FOUR

Remy took his first blissful sip of coffee and closed his eyes. These few stolen minutes each morning were worth their weight in gold. It wouldn't be long before those actors descended on his people. A snarl worked his throat. Why had he agreed to that nonsense? He wanted his people happy was why. Everyone deserved to find their mates.

He really hoped the director found his mate soon so the man could get out of his house. It wasn't that he begrudged sharing his home; it was his pack. They still felt the sting of Megan's scheme. Megan had used her own pride and tried to kill their partnership with the neighboring wolves by setting up a plan to kill the wolf pack alpha and his mate. She'd made their pride want to hide in shame. The pain she put the wolves and his lions through...well, she got what she deserved.

He'd watched his pride members closely to see if anyone was overly affected by her death. She had been his beta for a while and was close to many, but he didn't know of any blood family or romantic relationships.

Maybe these actors were actually the distraction the pride needed. The creaking sound of the front door opening had him reaching into the cabinet to pull out a couple additional coffee mugs. Bertha would just help herself, but the director might not be so pushy.

His lion jumped up and ran in a circle. It let out a roar so loud in his head, he cringed. Claws pushed against his skin wanting to get out. It took Remy a moment to figure out what was causing it. Then a scent hit him, vanilla and parchment paper. It was an odd smell but two he had always loved. But he wasn't attracted to men, so maybe the director brought an assistant and that was where the scent came from.

Their footsteps resonated closer as they moved through the house. Shock rooted him to the spot. His lion pushed him to move. The animal wanted out. He fidgeted from foot to foot, anxious to meet the owner of the scent but nervous. Damn Gerri for sending his mate over now when he asked her not to. He should have known she wouldn't listen and do what she thought best.

Bertha showed up first in his kitchen. "Remy, this is Genevieve or Gen. I like Gen." She gave an evil grin and pointed at someone that walked into his field of vision at that moment. "Genevieve, this surly bastard is our alpha, Remington Leandros, also known as Remy."

Remy's heart raced a million miles per second. His lion roared from within, wanting to be near his mate. He clenched his teeth and took a deep breath. Bad move. Her scent filled his lungs and he couldn't get enough of her. Fuck.

Remy shook his head, trying to stay in control and smiled at Genevieve. "Please, ignore Bertha. She is not the best representation of my lions. Call me Remy. No one but my mother calls me Remington and that was only when I was in trouble when I was young."

Bertha scoffed and flashed a toothy smile at them both. "Good thing you put a pot of coffee on. Gen, you want a cup? He won't get it for you, lazy bastard."

Remy closed his eyes and sighed. The need to touch Gen was overwhelming. How would she react if he picked her up, carried her to his room and tore that outfit off until he could lick every inch of her? She might have a problem with a random stranger doing that.

There was a quiet chuckle and opened his eyes to see Genevieve looking back and forth between the two of them. "It's a pleasure to meet you. I was going to offer you a cup of coffee. You may notice, Bertha, I have two extra cups laid out."

Gen stuck her hand out and Remy hesitated. He didn't want to touch his mate. He was afraid he wouldn't let go. Ever. She started to withdraw her hand and he saw sadness cross her face for a moment. Remy quickly grabbed her hand and his lion went crazy.

"Thank you, Remy. It's a pleasure to meet you as well."

Remy let go of her hand with a sigh and took a few steps back. He needed space from her scent and the softest skin he ever felt. Ah, for fuck's sakes. Who was he kidding? He needed her. Not distance. But damn it all to hell, she was human and he knew all about their need to get to know people before agreeing to be mates. As if there was a choice. He swallowed a growl and gestured to the kitchen table.

"Please, have a seat," then he grabbed his cup of coffee and sat across from Gen.

Gen gave him the sweetest smile and his chest filled with happiness. "Thank you, and I would love a cup of coffee, black, please. Remy, thank you for opening your house and your pride to my troupe. We really appreciate the opportunity to learn from the source."

Remy glanced over his shoulder at Bertha and then back to Gen. "*Your* troupe?"

She nodded.

"I'm sorry. I didn't realize you were the director. I made a stupid assumption." He shook his head in consternation and laughed at himself.

Bertha set a cup of coffee in front of Gen and then sat in the chair beside her. "Didn't I say bastard? Hmmm? Anyway, what are you looking for exactly from our pride?"

Gen picked up her cup of coffee and blew across the surface. Remy had to shift in his chair, his imagination running wild with those lips wrapped around his cock, blowing lightly and then licking the tip. He groaned and shifted again in his chair.

Gen's soft gaze swept over his face and he wanted to toss her over his shoulder and run to his bedroom with her, caveman style. Yeah, that would go so well. She glanced back to Bertha. "First, like Bertha, I like Gen too. It's easier. Second, the play we're doing is a fantasy-type piece. In no way is it realistic, but it's fun and different. My people need to see how lions interact with each other and humans in a normal setting. We would like to witness a shift if it's not too personal."

She paused and Remy assumed it was to gauge their reactions. He nodded, and she continued speaking. "We would like to see children and learn about them in relation to being a shifter. Honestly, they all have

21

questions that relate to the specific parts they play. I have questions about how you run the pride."

Bertha gave a sharp nod at him and drained her coffee cup. "I'll let you get acquainted and go check on the rest of the troupe. Gen, if you need me, just ask anyone for Bertha and they will direct you to me."

Gen smiled and Remy's heart jumped. She was stunning. Her smile lit up the whole room and he was lost.

"So really, thank you for letting us stay here. I'm sure it's not what you wanted to be dealing with."

"It's no problem, really. Things were getting a little boring around here. You've brought needed sunshine with you." For him anyway. "How did you get into theater and directing?"

She shrugged. "I was an only child growing up and my mother said that at a young age, I was acting out skits I made up. I put my dolls and stuffed animals in place and talked to them as if they were other actors on stage with me. Then when I got older, Mom told me I should study directing because I was so bossy."

He laughed and she smiled at her memories. "I can't imagine working anywhere else." She sipped her drink. "What about you? How long have you been the alpha?"

"My father died a year ago, then we moved

out here to the hills and forests. So, I'm relatively new at this, but I'd been assisting Dad for years so not much changed when I took over."

"Is your mother around?" she asked.

His mother was a touchy subject he didn't talk about with anyone. But Gen wasn't just anyone. "In the shifter world, lions mate for life. There is a bond that is unbreakable except by death. So, when one of the mates dies, the other is greatly affected. Many times, the single mate's mind starts to breakdown. When that happens, they can go rogue, but usually decide to join their mate in the afterlife."

Sadness and embarrassment filling her scent, Gen said, "I'm sorry for being nosy —"

"But my mom is no regular shifter," he added.

"Oh." Gen perked up at that.

"My mother is a strong alpha mate. She decided a while back to live away from the pack. I think that's her way of staying sane. She doesn't have the constant reminder of what she lost. Plus, the high-rise she lives in has 'sexy young men' catering to a bunch of old women. Or so she told me once." He shook his head.

Gen laughed. "That's good enough of a reason to me. Do you see her much?"

He sighed as he glanced down at the table. "Not as much as I'd like. I don't think she'll ever come back here. I kinda feel like I lost them both."

Gen rested her hand on his, and a thrill like no other ricocheted through him. His lion did backflips. He hadn't seen that before.

She said, "I know how you feel. I don't see my parents much either. Part of that is my fault, though. I stay so busy working, there's hardly any time to get away." Her thumb rubbed over the rough skin on the back of his hand.

His eyes locked onto hers. So beautiful. His mate. He could sit forever and get lost in her gaze. He felt as if he could see her soul reaching out to him. Boy, he needed to get a grip. It could be days before they mated. He'd be walking around with a constant hard-on, and that wouldn't be good. He couldn't imagine what Bertha would say about that.

Looking around, Remy was startled when realizing Bertha had left the room already and he was alone with Gen. He cleared his throat. "So, what do you know about shifters?" His lion was at attention, waiting to hear her response.

"Very little actually. I know pretty much all types of animals have shifters. The alpha is the leader...yeah, that's about it. What should I know?" Gen leaned forward with an eager smile on her face.

Remy ran his hand down his face and chuckled. "Do you know anything about fated mates?"

Gen shook her head and bit her lip. Remy

groaned and sat back in his chair. "How did you come to contact Gerri Wilder of the Paranormal Dating Agency to help you find a lion pride?"

Gen had a confused look on her face for a moment. "Oh, *Gerri*, yes. My assistant was put in contact with her. I honestly don't know how they met or planned this." Gen paused and glanced down at the table then back up to Remy. "Did you say Paranormal Dating Agency? Like she sets up people or shifters on dates?"

Remy chuckled and pushed his chair back from the table. "Let me show you where you will be staying. One of the pride brought your luggage in while we were chatting in the kitchen."

Remy waited for her to stand and then walked out of the kitchen. "Up the stairs, your room is the first door on the left. I'm across the hall from you. If you will excuse me for a few minutes, I need to talk to Bertha."

FIVE

Gen watched the hottest man she had ever seen walk out the front door and stared at his ass as he moved. Gerri Wilder was damn good if that was the type of men, or shifters, she set people up with.

She continued up the stairs and stopped in front of the door on the left side of the hall. She bit her lip and glanced at Remy's door across from her. She wanted to know more about the man. Was he married? Did he have children, or cubs? And how was he in bed? She groaned. She shouldn't be wanting to know those things, but she did.

Remy had sparked a sexual interest in her in the blink of an eye. That never happened. Not to Gen. She needed to stop the sexual thoughts.

She wasn't a ho. She was usually the chick guys dumped because she made them wait months getting to know each other before putting out. Talk about a major turnaround. She laughed to herself and opened the bedroom door.

The first thing she noticed was her suitcase on a large, four-poster bed. She stepped inside and closed the door behind her. Her feet sank into a plush carpet. The wall next to the door contained a dresser and across the room were two doors. She assumed one would be a closet and the other a bathroom.

Gen unzipped her suitcase and stuffed clothes into the dresser then glanced at the doors and randomly opened one. On the other side was the biggest bathroom she had ever seen. A sunken tub with enough room for three people, a double sink, and a shower stall with an oversized shower head. If this was the guest bathroom, she could only imagine what the master looked like.

She laughed and walked back into the bedroom, opening the other door to be sure it was the closet. She smiled and hung up the rest of her clothes. A few minutes later, she was done unpacking and unsure what to do now. Should she look for Remy? Check in on her friends? Or even walk around and meet the other shifters?

Gen left the bedroom and stared at Remy's door again. Checking the hall to make sure no one was watching, she leaned against the wood on the other side of the aisle. Even here, she could smell his woodsy scent. It sent her insides whirling. She wanted nothing more than to wrap him around her and snuggle. And screw his brains out. Yeah, okay. She was a slut. Was there such as thing as an entry level ho? Ugh. She needed to get her damn hormones under control.

But she had to curb her curiosity. He'd freak out if he knew she was having nasty thoughts about him minutes after they met. Besides, what if there was a Mrs. Leandros? That would be embarrassing.

She went downstairs and called out to see if Remy was in the house. No one answered, so she went to the front door and stepped outside. She debated locking the door or just shutting it. "You can shut it. We don't lock our doors around here."

Gen jumped and turned to the voice. In front of her stood a tall, gorgeous man. Was it a prerequisite for shifters to be hot? "Oh, thanks, I'm Gen. The director of the play and troupe that invaded your pride." The man laughed and stepped closer to her "Nice to meet you. I'm Jensen."

Gen gave a small smile and stepped away from Remy's door, looking around. "I was going to walk around and check in with my friends to see how they settled in. Do you know where they are staying?" Jensen nodded and turned, his broad body looming way too close to her. For some reason, he didn't give her the knots in her belly that Remy did. Huh? Go figure. "I can show you. Do you mind if I ask a few questions while we walk?"

"Not at all. As long as I can ask you a few at the same time." Gen laughed. This could turn into a game of twenty questions.

Jensen smiled and matched her pace, slowing down to stroll down the path alongside her. "Can you tell me about the play you're performing?"

Gen glanced at the ground and hesitated. "I don't want to offend you. The play is a local artist's attempt and he made a huge donation to the theater if we performed it."

Gen paused and looked at Jensen out of the corner of her eye. "Anyway, the lead actor is a lion shifter, who happens to be an astronaut. He finds true love the week before he is to go on a month-long space mission. He brings his woman to his pride and the rest is basically him introducing her to a pride and shifters."

Jensen started laughing and stopped in his tracks. "That sounds interesting."

Gen turned to face Jensen and put her hands on her hips. "How bad is the premise?" He wiped his cheeks off, and Gen wasn't sure if he was actually laughing or crying or teasing her.

"I honestly don't know a lion who would be comfortable away from his mate for a month, the pull would be strong. We don't actually call them true love but fated mates. Our animals know instantly when we meet them, and they push until we have completed the mating bond." Gen tried not to blush at his insinuation. "As for the lion wanting to go to outer space...well, most animals prefer to keep their feet on the ground unless they are the flying types."

They continued strolling for a minute and Gen pondered what he said. "I can't change the basics of the play, but can you tell me more about mates? I can make sure that part is as authentic as possible."

Jensen nodded, his smile not quite reaching his eyes. She wondered if she'd said something she shouldn't have. Maybe the play wasn't really up to real shifter standards. "Tell me what you want to know."

"Can a shifter date while they wait to find their mate? Can they fall in love with someone who isn't their mate?" Gen hoped she wasn't coming across as too forward or make Jensen think she was interested because she wasn't. Well, not in him, at least.

Remy was a whole other story. That man made her blood sing and her mouth water.

Jensen smirked and his eyes did a quick flash of color. She wasn't sure what that was about. "Of course, we can. We fall in love and date like humans. But we can only ever have children with our fated mate. The one person who is made for us."

Gen looked at the cabins that were getting closer with each step. "I have one more question for you. If you fall in love with someone who isn't your mate, what happens when you finally do meet your other half?"

"Some shifters will only date shifters because they know the score. They know at any moment one of them could meet their mate and it would be over."

"Over?" Gen asked, her blood turning cold. Could someone end a good relationship like that for a new person because they're fated?

"Yes. Fated mates are born to be together. If someone tells you that you're their fated mate, then their world will revolve around you. They will live to make you happy because you have brought them a love that transcends death."

"Wow," Gen murmured, "sounds serious."

"It sorta is," Jensen replied. "The males won't look at other women. Some go as far as not even want to be in the same room as other females. Your fated mate will only crave you and want to be near you always. He's your ultimate lover and perfect match."

"Seems pretty ideal," she sighed dreamily. "How do I snag myself one?" She laughed to show she was joking, but inside she really wanted someone like that. Someone who would love her only and not flirt with every woman in the cast.

Gen shook her head to get the memory of her last couple relationships from her brain. She'd come to the realization that no man could keep it in his pants when a pretty face walked by. Even if he was holding her hand at the time. Maybe she had been looking in the wrong place.

If a shifter were to fall in love with her, she'd give him a chance, no questions asked. But she'd have to keep her heart to herself if they weren't fated. Knowing her sucky luck, she'd fall for one shifter after another who would find their fated mates shortly after she fell in love. Great. Now her heart hurt.

Jensen continued, "Some choose to live with the person they fall in love with, fated mate or not." He just confirmed what she feared. She would only want her fated mate.

"Those shifters don't look for their mate, or don't believe they will ever find that one person and take happiness any way they can." Jensen stared off into space and Gen watched him. Had that happened to him? Had he lost a love to someone who found their fated one? That would suck big time and it made her feel a little sad for him. "Anyway, your friends are in those cabins."

Gen smiled at him. "Thank you for showing me the way and answering my questions. I really appreciate your help."

Gen spotted Bertha waving at her. "Your assistant told me we were expecting one more arrival, the new leading lady. Do you know when she is coming?"

Gen had forgotten about the new actress. She was just given the position the day before. "No, but I will find out and get back to you. Do you have room for her?" Bertha waved away her words and turned the other direction and walked off.

"Were you warned about Bertha's interesting personality?" Jensen was laughing and Gen couldn't stop herself from joining in.

"Yes, she is quite entertaining. But I assume I should find out when the new actress will arrive."

Jensen cocked his head to the side. "What happened that you had to get a new actress? Doesn't each spot in the play have an understudy?"

Gen sighed and glanced at the cabins. "Yes, but when our female lead had to move away suddenly, I felt her understudy wasn't ready for the spotlight yet. So, we held auditions and picked a new leading lady. Thanks again for the help. I'll see you later."

Gen walked to one of the cabins and knocked. She wasn't sure who stayed in which cabin, but she wanted to check on all of them.

SIX

Remy marched out the front door thinking about his mate. He had to find Bertha to see what the real story was. It only took a minute to locate her. Her voice was stronger than her scent.

"Bertha," he called out. "We need to talk."

She stood by a group of the theater people, listening while they talked to his lions. Some seemed nervous and others were asking questions and chatting away.

Bertha sighed and waved him over. "Fine, Alpha Surly. What do you want to talk about?"

Remy shook his head in exasperation and took a few steps away, knowing Bertha would follow. "Why did you bring Gen here? Did you know she was my mate?" Remy ran his fingers through his hair in frustration. "Our pride needs me to be strong and focused. I don't have time to date a human mate." Remy growled and Bertha stepped closer to him. "You know they're a lot more temperamental and difficult than shifters."

"Don't get crabby with me, boy. I was there when you were born, and alpha or not, I will bend you over my knee." Bertha patted his cheek with a grin to take the sting out of her words then continued, "Yes, I knew your mate was among the crew of the theater. Gerri told me that much. I didn't know who it was, though.

"There are a few women here, the leading lady from what I overhead was just cast and will be here soon. The understudy for her role, the leading man, his understudy, and a few other minor characters and crew are staying with us." Bertha glanced over her shoulder at the cast mingling with his lions and turned back to him.

He slid his fingers through his hair in frustration. "I didn't mean to get testy with you. I can't divide my attention between my mate and this pack, though. They need my full attention. I'm the only one who can pull them out of this lull we're in. Megan caused a lot of distress; we need to rise above it." Remy sighed and watched his lions.

They laughed and were generally having a good time. Quite a few of them he hadn't seen smile in a long while. "Megan took men from us and they haven't all returned fully. What she put them and us through... Well, we need time to heal the wounds." Remy glanced down at Bertha to gauge her reaction.

"My boy, you take too much on your shoulders. Do not let your personal pride get in the way of what our lion pride needs. They will heal, and these actors might be the distraction we all need. Look at how happy they are already!

"We're having a potluck feast in the courtyard tonight. Maybe you can ask Gen to put on a spontaneous show. Hell, invite Azai and Dalissa to come over. It's been too long." Bertha smiled at him and then wandered away.

He laughed out loud and quietly called to her. "Careful or the others will know you aren't as crazy as you pretend."

Bertha cackled loudly as she kept walking. Remy shook his head and moved toward his pride and guests. He wanted to introduce himself and see if his lions were having as much fun as it appeared. They were laughing and joking around, the somber mood that had shrouded everyone might finally be lifting.

He watched as Augustus smiled at a young woman who stood just outside the group. She kept glancing around then looking back at the ground. She seemed really shy, or her body language appeared that way.

Augustus bit his lip and took a step closer before one of the actors asked him a question. He turned but kept glancing at the woman. Remy wondered if Gerri really had sent a few mates to the pride.

"Hello, everyone, I just wanted to introduce myself and make sure you were settling in okay. My name is Remy. I am the pride's leader or alpha." Remy smiled at each person and hoped they were comfortable enough to chat with him.

Augustus stepped toward the alpha. "Remy, let me introduce you to the actors who are staying with us. This is Jerome. He is the leading man in their production." Jerome nodded and stuck his hand out to Remy. "Next to him is Bailey. She is the understudy to the leading lady and has two other parts. Did I get that right, Bailey?"

The woman smiled and nodded, but Remy noticed a tightening of her eyes. Something Augustus said didn't sit well with her.

"I'm James, just a random small part in the play but I do a lot of the stage set up and build props. I wanted to learn as much as I can, so I asked to tag along." James smiled sheepishly at August. Remy wasn't sure if it was because he didn't wait to be introduced or if he was afraid of how he would be introduced.

Augustus gestured to the young woman who stood slightly apart from everyone else. "This is Shelby. I'm told she is quite amazing when she gets on stage." He glanced at her and mumbled, "I can't wait to see it." Remy was sure no one but he and Star heard his whisper. "Last, but not least, is Ethan."

Remy shook hands with each person and smiled. He wanted them at ease and comfortable with his people. "Did anyone tell you about the potluck we are having tonight?"

Not surprisingly, James was the first to speak up. "Bertha mentioned it when we first arrived. We kinda feel bad we don't have anything to bring to the feast."

Remy's smile grew bigger. "There's no need. This pride is happy to feed everyone. We work together and share. You are more than welcome to anything here."

A tiny voice blurted out, "Are you really feeding us freshly caught Bambi?"

Remy glanced over to see Shelby looking at him from under her lashes. "I'm sure someone will bring the meat, but we will have hamburgers, hot dogs, even chicken, along with traditional sides you would expect. It's a potluck. We eat just like anyone else." He saw Shelby take a deep breath and noticed a few of the others did the same. "Let me guess— Bertha?"

Star wrapped her arm around Shelby's shoulder. "She was just teasing you. She's a bit special and we just go along with it. Bertha is one of the most loyal people you will ever meet."

Remy heard footsteps behind him and glanced back to see Gen walking over. "I was wondering where everyone was. I stopped by the cabins." Remy smiled and waited for her to get closer. "Gen, meet Star and Augustus. They've been playing tour guide to your troupe."

Gen smiled and then looked back to him. "I met Jensen. He showed me to the cabins and explained about mates. Sounds like the script is going to need some tweaking already."

"Gen, did you hear about the potluck tonight? Remy assured us there will be more than just meat they caught." Ethan shuddered.

Gen tilted her head. "Ethan, where do you think the food we buy in stores comes from?"

Ethan snorted. "A factory that adds all kinds of preservatives and shit. I know it's bad for you, but I NEED that."

Remy covered a laugh with a cough at his theatrics. "We'll eat in about an hour. Is there anything you need before then?" Everyone shook their head and started to wander off.

Gen called out to Bailey. "Leslie will be here shortly since she missed the ride this morning. Can you show her around and get her caught up with what's going on, please?"

Remy watched as the younger woman smiled and nodded. Something was wrong there. She was polite but Remy could smell deceit. He wasn't sure what it was about yet, though. He started to walk over to Gen when he noticed Jerome hung back also. He turned away so he didn't appear to be eavesdropping, but shifter hearing meant he could walk away and still hear everything they said.

"Hey, Gen, are you all settled up at the big house?"

Gen smiled absently at him. "Yeah, I'm good. Everything okay with you guys? Anything I need to know about?"

Remy waited impatiently. He didn't think they would have any problems, but he wanted to be the first to know. "No, everything's great so far. The lions are answering questions and are being very friendly with everyone." Jerome looked down at the ground then up at Gen. "Can I pick you up and walk you to the potluck?"

Gen swung her head to look at Jerome. "Are you serious? I told you to stop flirting. There isn't anything going on with us. Besides, Remy already offered to show me around tonight so it will be easier to just go with him."

Remy puffed his chest out. His lion was proud she chose him, even if it was a small lie. He walked over to where they stood. "Gen, ready to get the tour now? We have time before the potluck."

Remy wanted to warn the other man to back the fuck off, but he couldn't appear too interested yet. Gen looked up at him with a smirk and he wondered what she thought was humorous.

SEVEN

Gen silently laughed as she listened to Remy. She wondered if he knew he was growling. It was like a combination of a rumble and a purr. She supposed it was to warn off others, but it was so cute.

Jerome hurried toward the cabins and Remy looked at her. "So, about that tour...are you still up for it? Or were you just saying that to chase the eager puppy away?"

Gen couldn't control the snort laugh that came out. He was an eager puppy. It was a great description. "I would love a tour. I'm excited to meet more of your pride tonight, too. I've learned so much and I hope my troupe is learning stuff, too."

"So, what did you learn about mates?"

Gen glanced at Remy as they started walking. "Well, each shifter has one, and some settle for companionship until they find theirs. You can only have children with your fated mate, though. Did I miss anything?"

Remy pointed to a trail in the woods. "That path takes you over to the wolves whose land borders ours. You will meet Azai and Dalissa later." He dragged his feet through the leaves and Gen followed along. "No, you summed up mates well. Did Jensen tell you that shifters can mate with other types of shifters *and* humans?"

Gen wasn't sure why he was telling her this information. It really didn't matter to her play but with the male character falling in love with a human, it made sense to her. "The female lead is human, so I assumed it was possible." Gen smiled to let him know she was teasing. "Tell me about your pride. I sense a sadness among them, just under the surface."

Remy paused and stared off for a minute. "That's a long story. Are you sure you want to hear it?" Gen wanted to know everything about Remy. She had the feeling he was going to be important to her in the future. It helped he was hot as hell and she wanted to jump his bones.

"I've got all the time you need. Maybe it will help me with the play, maybe it's just for me." She smiled at him and ducked her head. She didn't want to come across as forward, but he intrigued her. Did he feel it, too?

Probably not, she thought, that would make her his mate and he would have told her, right? Everyone looked for their mate and wanted that connection. It only made sense he would say something if it were true. It had to be wishful thinking on her part.

"Alphas of the pride normally have a beta, or a second-in-command. Mine was a lion named Megan." Remy stopped and pointed off to the left.

"Down through the woods leads to a stream, I'll take you there sometime." Gen smiled. Was he planning a future date or just changing the subject for a moment?

"Anyway, Megan, well, she was evil. But she hid it for a long time. We didn't expect how crazy she was until a few months ago.

"She thought lions were the best and biggest shifter. Everyone else should bow to us. The pride took her betrayal hard. We lost our sense of safety, trust in each other, and morale has been low. Today was the first time I saw happiness from any of them. We have you to thank for that."

"I'm not sure we've done that much since we just arrived. But everybody seems to be getting along. What seems to be the problem?"

He shoved his hands into his pockets. "It's hard to explain."

"Are they less active than before? Have you noticed a decline in socializing? Are they eating less? Even complaining less?" she asked.

He stopped and stared at her. "Yes, yes, yes and yes, how'd you know all that?"

She smiled at his adorable shocked expression. "Part of being a director is understanding human nature. I direct my actors to be as real to life as possible. You might be shifters, but you're half human and deal with the same things regular people do." She continued walking. She liked being close to him. How could she make him feel the same way?

"Sounds like you're speaking from experience, too," he commented.

Damn, he was observant. She couldn't hide anything from him. She looked away. "Like everyone else, I've suffered heartache, disappointment, and joy. I've gone through bouts of depression before. Dark times where I wondered why I was alive." Why was she telling him this? He'd think she was a whacko and avoid her. But he was so easy to talk to. She felt like he really cared about what she was saying.

Next she knew, her face was smashed into a wonderful smelling, very muscular chest. Remy's arms wrapped around her, cocooning her in comfort. His hot breath tickled her ear.

"Don't you ever think that you're not wanted, not loved. You have a purpose on this planet, and I—" he stuttered over his words then shut his mouth.

She pushed back from him and stared into his eyes. "You what?" He was going to say something important. She felt it in her soul.

"I hope I'm there when you find that purpose," he said slowly. Her heart flipped. What did he mean by that? Was he saying he wanted to be around her? His line of sight dropped to her lips. God, she wanted him to kiss her. His head dipped lower.

A loud throat clearing jarred her from her romance-soaked brain. She looked up and realized they were back at Remy's house. Standing by the porch was Bertha and her new leading lady, Leslie.

"Hey, Leslie, glad you made it. Did you get settled in okay?"

Leslie opened her mouth, glanced at Bertha, and shut it again.

"Leslie, here, got a welcome message on her bed in the cabin."

Leslie gaped at Bertha, and Gen sighed. "I'm assuming it wasn't a nice kind of welcome based on her reaction." Leslie shook her head frantically. Bertha stared at Remy who nodded. Were they having a silent conversation? Gen glanced between them, waiting for someone to fill her in on the welcome left for her star.

After a minute, neither spoke, so Gen wrapped her arm around Leslie. "Why don't you come up to my room, take a hot bath and relax. I'll find out what's going on and we can get you sorted. Is that okay with you?" Leslie nodded and glanced over her shoulder at Remy. He watched them go inside but didn't say anything.

* * *

Fifteen minutes later, Gen went back downstairs to find Remy waiting for her and Bertha gone. "All right, are you going to tell me what that was all about?"

Remy gave her a funny look. "Are you referring to the welcome message? Because I don't know much. Do you want to go to the cabin and check it out with me?"

"Lead the way to the cabin, but tell me about the looks between you and Bertha. Were you two actually having a conversation?"

Remy looked at her in surprise. "I'm sorry. I didn't realize you weren't aware members of the same pack or pride can telepathically speak to each other. It helps when we are shifted and out for a run or a hunt.

"Bertha was telling me what they found. Leslie was shaken up, so she didn't want to talk about it in front of her." As they neared the cabin, Gen began to worry about what they would find. "Bertha is waiting inside. We sent the rest of the ladies to the potluck with Star."

Gen walked into the cabin and paused while her eyes adjusted to the dim light. Bertha stood toward the back of the big room. The cabin had four beds and a dresser next to each. The room also contained a table and chairs. "Wow, kinda plain cabins. Not really what I was expecting." Gen tried to smother her laugh. She had a huge bed, a walk-in closet, and a sunken tub.

"These cabins aren't normally used. We haven't been here long, and with everything that went down, finishing the renovations on these buildings...well, they were put on hold. We figured beds were the most important thing for your people. The bathroom is completely updated, though, if that helps. The pride is taking turns feeding everyone. This gives your people a chance to meet and talk to the lions in smaller settings, too." What he said made sense and no one had complained so far to her.

Bertha apparently was done waiting on them because she yelled out, "Are you lovebirds done? We got shit to take care of." Remy sighed and walked over to the bed Bertha stood in front of.

"Where's the note she found?"

Bertha grunted and pointed at the table. Remy glanced over and then looked back to the bed. Gen saw the dark wet spot on the blanket and she really didn't want to know what it was from.

She crossed to the table and picked up the note. *You don't belong here.* Gen gasped and dropped the note. Remy rushed to her side.

"Are you okay?"

Gen nodded and stared at the note. "I don't understand. Why would someone send Leslie a note like that?" Remy picked it up and read over the message.

EIGHT

Remy set the note on the table and turned back to the bed. "Bertha, what was on the bed and where was the note found?"

Bertha glanced at Gen, then back at him. He nodded to her to discuss it aloud. "I met Leslie at her car and escorted her here. When we came in, the others were outside chatting. Everyone seemed pleasant enough.

"I showed Leslie inside and which bed was open for her. Lying on the pillow was the note and below it was a gutted rabbit. I asked and no one saw anyone come in who wasn't supposed to, and the scents were the humans and our lions. No one out of place or unexpected." Bertha scowled at the bed like it could tell her exactly what she wanted to know.

"So, you're saying it was one of my people or your lions who did this? But why?" Gen looked so lost and confused, his lion was pushing for him to comfort his mate.

"There are other possibilities; someone could have masked their scent and entered the cabin. For now, we need to interview Leslie and go to the potluck and pretend all is well. We will just watch everyone tonight."

Remy glanced at Bertha and then back to Gen. "Gen, let's check on Leslie and escort her to the potluck. We don't want her first impressions of lions to be dead rabbits."

Bertha cackled a bit too loudly but didn't say anything else. Gen glanced around the room briefly. "I'm going to check in with my people first, then we can go. If that's okay with you?" Remy nodded and watched her walk out of the room.

"Are you going to tell her she is your mate or are you going to pretend she's not? Someone tonight will spill the beans, and you know it. This pack has been waiting for you to find the one for a long time." Bertha never pulled punches, and this was no exception. But how did he broach the topic of forever mates when her leading lady was getting threats? It seemed tactless to do now.

"Yes, when the time is right. But more importantly, we need to know who sent that note. What are your thoughts?" Remy relied on

Bertha's insight. Too many people, including their pack mates, treated Bertha like she was crazy, but she was smart. She just didn't bother to spare anyone's feelings.

"Leslie could have an enemy, but I really think that is unlikely. It could be someone protesting the play. It's common knowledge the play is about shifters and we both know how radical people can get. It could be related to Megan. We don't know if she was working alone, she could have had sympathizers in the pride. There are too many possibilities at this point to make a guess."

Remy hung his head. She was right. The only thing they could do was watch and wait. "Okay. I'm going to walk my mate home. See you in a bit." Remy couldn't help the smile that graced his face as he said those two words, *my mate*. He walked a bit taller, shoulders squared, just because she was near.

He wanted to impress her and make her love him. "Remy, mates are a wonderful thing, but they take work. Fate matches us but hard work and communication are what keep you together. Remember that and you will do fine." Bertha kissed him on the cheek then walked out the door. "Besides, if it didn't work out, sex isn't that important to you, right?"

Remy rolled his eyes. She thought she was funny, but who didn't like sex? With that thought, he walked outside to see Gen talking to one of the actresses. His lion roared in approval, he liked her and wanted more. And he wanted it now! He took a few steps toward Gen when he saw her glance over with an odd look. He rushed closer, needing to know what distressed his mate.

"Is everything okay, Gen?"

The understudy glanced at him and narrowed her eyes for a moment then smiled. "Hi. Remy, right? I'm Bailey. Leslie's understudy and another minor part in the play. I was just telling Gen that I called Leslie to check on her and she said she was fine. Though she wasn't sure she wanted to stay on the cast. I volunteered to take her spot, since I am the understudy and all."

Remy was speechless. Was this woman trying to claim the leading lady spot before the actress even quit? And what the hell was the look she shot him when he walked up?

"Hi, yes, Bailey. I remember you. Would you mind if I stole Gen for a bit before the potluck? We have a few things to talk about and I'm sure she would like to check on Leslie." He nodded goodbye to her and wrapped his arm around Gen's back. With a gentle tug, he got her walking and they headed to his home.

"Remy, did we bring your pride more drama? This is the last thing you need. I'm so sorry."

Remy stopped and turned Gen to face him.

He ran his hand up her arm to cup her cheek, then pulled her closer to his chest. "I don't care what you might have brought with you, who you brought with you, or even why you are here. I am thankful you stepped onto my land. Who knows how long it would have taken me to find you, otherwise?"

He sighed and licked his lips. "You're mine. My mate. My only. I won't let you go."

Gen's brows drew down. He wanted to kiss each one. He watched her beautiful face as thoughts went through her head. Was it too soon? Hell, he'd known her for mere hours and now he'd told her he wanted forever. No problem for shifters. But humans didn't work that way. Especially human females. Then he saw a light twinkle in her blue irises.

She rose on her toes. "Good, because I was afraid something was wrong with me. Will you kiss me now?" Remy laughed and leaned forward, brushing his lips against hers. The briefest of touches, but he had to know what her lips felt like.

He lifted his head and waited to see her reaction. "That wasn't enough for me." Gen laughed and wrapped her arms around his neck, pulling his head to her lips. He kissed the corner of her mouth, then lightly pressed a kiss to the other side before gently pressing his lips against hers.

Gen moaned and opened her mouth. Remy

angled his head, so he could take the kiss deeper. Their tongues dueled and he couldn't tell who moaned, but the sound made his cock rock hard. He rubbed his cock against the juncture of her thighs. This was getting too heavy too fast.

"Remy, don't stop, please." Gen wrapped her legs around his waist, and he groaned. He felt her heat through both their jeans, his cock throbbed with need.

"Leslie is in your room and I want you to scream when you come. We need to stop for now, but after the potluck, you will be mine in every sense of the word." Remy pushed his lion down and promised they would fuck their mate soon. Time was not in their favor right now, and he heard people talking as they walked along the path.

"Come on, my love, let's check on Leslie and get ready for an impromptu party."

NINE

Fuck. No one ever said lions would be a cock teaser, or in this case, a vagina blocker. Didn't they have a name when a man blocked a woman from getting some? But he was right. They were in the open, but the thought of getting caught was enticing. Remy might not feel the same, but—holy shit—they were mates.

This explained the strong attraction she had to him. She felt the pull but dismissed it to going too long without sex. "What does this mean for me as a human to be your mate? Will my life be altered? I mean, Jensen explained mates and what they mean to shifters, but what does it mean to humans?"

Remy walked and grabbed her hand, sending tingles down her back. "When we are mated, and by that I mean I have given you the mate mark, some humans gain the ability to shift into the animal their mate is. The only other changes would be things humans go through when they get married. The mate mark is more binding than a marriage certificate in our world."

Remy kept walking, but she could see him glancing at her every few steps. She had to be honest with herself, this was a bit more than she expected. It felt right, but marriage, even shifter marriage, seemed like a big step. No one had made her feel like he did. She could trust him in a group of naked women—something she'd never do with a human male.

"So, I could still work at the theater? I need my job. I'm not going to depend on you. Would I move in with you here? What about your lions? Will they accept me since I'm human?" Remy halted them on the porch of his home and pulled her to him again.

"Love, of course you can still work. Only if you want to, though. You will never want for anything again. I want you by my side every minute of every day and in my bed every night. Of course, I want you to move in with me. As for your last question, wait and see tonight." Remy hugged her and nipped at her ear. "Now let's get Leslie and have a small chat before we eat."

Gen inhaled Remy's unique scent, her

pussy clenching in need. Remy growled and whispered in her ear, "I can smell your lust. Tonight, I will fuck you senseless then do it all over again."

Gen's legs started to shake, and she stepped back from Remy. He was too potent; she needed a little space, or she was going to be all over him, screw privacy. The door opened and Leslie popped her head out. "I heard your voices. Is everything okay? Do you know what's going on?"

For a few minutes, Gen had forgotten about the rabbit and the note. Remy took all her attention and she wouldn't regret that. She wanted to focus on his lickable ass. Gen wrapped her arm around Leslie's shoulders. "Let's go in and talk for a few minutes. We have a couple questions for you before we go to dinner."

Gen heard Remy following them inside and when she sat at the kitchen table, he pulled his chair close to her and sat. "Leslie, I'm Remy, the alpha of this lion pride. I wish we could have met under better circumstances but is it okay if we ask you a few questions?"

Leslie lifted her tear-filled eyes and nodded. "Have you ever dated a shifter before? Is there someone who would be upset you came here this week?" Leslie stared at him as he asked the questions.

Gen glanced at Remy then studied Leslie to

see her response. "Are you thinking I'm the reason the note and animal were left behind? I don't understand why I was targeted. Yes, I have dated shifters before, but it was casual hook-ups until they found their mates.

"No hard feelings. We knew it was temporary. I haven't actually been seeing anyone for a couple months now, so I have no idea why me." Gen sat back in her chair and silently groaned. This meant it had to do with the pack itself, or the theater group and Leslie was just bad timing.

Remy grumbled and the sound was definitely coming from his lion. Leslie jerked in her seat and looked at her with scared eyes.

"Leslie, would you accompany me to the potluck? I could use some help carrying out all the meat I just skinned." Leslie gasped and stared at Bertha who materialized in the kitchen.

"Where did you come from, and skinned meat?" Gen was sure Leslie was biting back the urge to vomit. "Bertha, I asked you to stop scaring the theater people. I promise you, Leslie, nothing being served tonight is unusual. It's all meat bought at a grocery store."

Gen smothered her laugh and watched Bertha. She had an evil twinkle in her eye. "Fine, I didn't skin the meat this time, but you can help me carry the food anyway. Get up, girl. I don't have all day to wait on you." Leslie looked a bit bewildered but jumped up to follow Bertha out the front door.

"I can see what you mean about Bertha. She is just what Leslie needs right now." Gen laughed out loud. "She's quite the character and not nearly as daft as she pretends. I like her."

Remy turned in his chair and placed his knees on either side of hers. "*My mate.* I love saying that. It sounds like Leslie was in the wrong place at the wrong time. It doesn't seem to be personal based on her responses. Do you have any ideas?"

Gen licked her lips and glanced at Remy's knees boxing her in. She leaned forward until they were touching. "None that help right now, but you're not helping sitting so close to me."

Remy chuckled, lifted her off the chair and onto his lap. "I have an idea what's on your mind." Gen opened her mouth to reply, but he beat her to it. His tongue swept into her mouth, brushing across hers. One of them moaned, but she wasn't sure who.

She wrapped her arms around his neck and kissed him with every ounce of passion she possessed. At the taste of him, a strange sensation centered in her lower belly, and her skin felt hot and tingly. A ball of need formed, and the punch was unlike anything she'd ever felt.

Maybe having the hots for a powerful, lick-worthy alpha drove her sex-o-meter to

DEFCON ten. He kissed her hungrily and demandingly on her throat, working his way to her breasts. He tongued her nipple through her shirt, drawing the hard peak into his mouth. Gen arched back, pushing her breasts up.

"Gen, tell me to stop now or I'm taking you to my bedroom and we will be very, very late to the potluck."

Gen looked into his eyes. "Why stop you? I want this as much as you do."

TEN

"Gen," he kissed down her neck, "let me love you.

"Remy..." she whispered.

"God, baby. I've been dying to slide inside you. I need you. I have to have you." He cupped her jaw as he stood and lifted her into his arms, her legs wrapping around his waist. "You're fucking gorgeous."

She snaked her tongue over his bottom lip and blinked, her gaze locking on his mouth. "I'll debate with you later on who's the most gorgeous. All I can think about is watching your head drop between my legs."

He leaned her against the wall and let her legs slide to the floor before taking her mouth again. Fuck, she was making him crazy. He yanked down her pants and slid a hand under her panties. *Ah, yes!* She was soaked. A rough breath left his chest. Her cream coated her underwear, making him ache.

He dropped to his knees and pushed her legs apart. There was no waiting. He needed this. He tore her underwear off in a rush and loved how fucking sexy she looked standing there, her pussy open for his view. At first, he kissed the inside of her trembling thighs and listened to her suck in a few shaky breaths. Yes. That's exactly what he wanted. To make her lose control quickly. He skated his tongue over her clit and her hands gripped his hair so hard, it stung.

Fuck, that only made him harder. Flattening his tongue, he pressed hard on her entrance and flicked up and down, gliding it over her slick pussy. The sweet taste of her essence coated his tongue.

She moaned, gasping for air. "Oh god! Oh, please. More." She said the words so softly; he almost didn't hear them. But he did. He heard the desperation and the need in her tone. And by fuck, that just made him lose any semblance of control. He licked faster, rising and falling and covering her pussy with his tongue down to the rim of her asshole and up to her clit.

Her little pleasure nub became hard with desire. Her thigh draped over his shoulder as he held her against the wall. She tensed, her rocking no longer smooth. Faster. Faster. Her gasps and moans grew shorter and breathier. Then she pressed her pussy tightly to his face and a soft scream held her still as her pussy gushed her sweet cream on his tongue.

She was fucking divine. Heaven couldn't taste this good. Lick after lick, he drank her in. She was sweet as honey. He was hooked even more if that was possible. He already didn't want another woman, another taste of anyone ever again. She was it. It was a matter of taking what was already his. "You're so fucking sweet, my Gen. Tasty. Like candy."

"Oh, god," she groaned.

"I can't wait to take you upstairs. I want inside you."

She pulled away from him and he stood, his face covered in her pussy juices. He licked his lips and she blinked hazily. That look of absolute pleasure on her face wasn't one he'd ever forget. Not in this lifetime. She curled her fingers into his T-shirt and pulled him to her.

"I like how I taste on you." She grinned. "But I'll love how you feel in me." She slid her hands down to his jeans. There was a soft hiss of the zipper going down and then his pants fell south. His heart was taking a beating. She was the only woman who had ever done that to him. She leaned forward and licked his neck, running her hand down his chest to his cock.

His breath choked in his lungs the moment

her hand was on his dick. It was like being home. She grasped his cock and caressed his hardness like she owned it. She did own it. Owned him, all of him. He tugged at her shirt and slid it over her head, wanting to see the rest of his beauty naked. He already loved it.

Every one of her curves made her perfect to fuck. Perfect to keep. Perfect to mate. Her black lacy bra contrasted against the paleness of her flesh. Her chest rose and fell with each of her breaths. "Like what you see?"

He met her gaze and pushed her against the kitchen wall. "I'll like it better when I'm fucking you, baby."

Lust filled her eyes. "I want you. All of you in me." He slid his fingers into her hair and lifted her leg, curling it around his waist as he prodded his cock into her entrance. Their gazes still locked, he pressed forward, his cock gliding into her and stretching her channel. Her eyes closed for a brief second while her body adjusted to his size. She dug her nails into his shoulders and swallowed hard.

"I have a thing for your tight little pussy."

She mewled. Her tiny whimper made his cock jerk. He fucking loved it. Loved knowing he was the one making her legs quiver and her pussy slicken. With one hand on her thigh, he yanked down her bra and her tit popped free above the bra cup. Her hard nipple made his mouth water. "I'm going to fuck you hard, baby," he said.

She grinned and pushed her chest forward, tugging his head down so he could lick her nipple. "When I walk out of here, I'm going to have something good to remember."

He gave a harsh laugh. "If you can walk out of here, I haven't fucked you hard enough." Remy groaned, thinking about everyone knowing she was his, his scent all over her body. Every movement she made when they left this kitchen would remind her she was his, and nothing would change that.

His cock pulled out of her slowly and immediately pressed back in, filling her with his hardness. God, she felt so good. He sucked her nipple hard as he drove in and out of her. Her pussy sucked at his cock, clasping around his length.

"Say you will stay with me," he mumbled at her breast while thrusting into her. She clung to him, unable to do anything but grip his shoulders and take every hard pounding he gave her. His cock felt like a branding rod, marking her as his from the very depths of her.

"There's no way I'm leaving you. You're my mate, and I have so much to learn about your world. You have me now and forever." He pounded into her again, and she yelled out with the force of her orgasm. He hiked her legs up higher and pushed in as deeply as he could, groaning as he spilled his seed into her. "Mine.

Mine. Only mine."

A few moments of heaving breaths by both and Remy lifted his head from her shoulder. "How about a quick shower before we join everyone outside? I'm sure the party has started without us."

Gen smiled and sighed. "I can't walk yet. My legs are putty."

ELEVEN

"**I** can take care of that problem." He wrapped his arms around her back and pulled her away from the wall. Gen laughed as he carried her up the stairs and into his bedroom. He walked into the shower and turned the water on. She gasped when the cold hit her back. "I'm sorry." Remy turned them so the cold water hit him and then reached back to adjust the temp.

She unwrapped her legs from his waist and took a step back. "Where's the soap or body wash?" Gen spotted everything in the corner of the shower and bent slightly to pick up a loofah. She felt Remy moved up behind her and press his erect cock into her ass cheeks. "Damn, woman, how am I supposed to control myself when you present me with a view like that?"

Gen looked at him over her shoulder. "Why should you control yourself?"

Remy groaned and rubbed his body against hers. "After the potluck, I will bend you over the bed and take you exactly like this."

Gen stood and turned to face him, brushing her breasts against his chest. "You are a tease, but I love the anticipation of what is to come. Now, let me wash your body." Remy growled and stepped back, his eyes glowing with a stunning yellow. "What does that mean? When your eyes turn yellow?" Gen poured the body wash on the loofah and started rubbing Remy's chest while she waited for him to respond to her query.

"My lion wants to come out and play with you."

Gen paused and stared up at him. "Oh, that wasn't what I was expecting." She bit her lip and continued rubbing the loofah across his chest to his arms and down to his hand, then repeated the process on the other side. "Could I play with him sometime? I mean, I want to see all of you, and this is a huge part of you." Gen chuckled as she thought about her word play, huge. Yes, that described a whole lot of Remy.

She ran her soapy hand down his stomach, circled his cock and squeezed tightly. "Are you washing my dick or playing with me?" Remy's voice came out with a growl and Gen felt her juices run down her thighs.

"I was only making sure you were squeaky clean." Gen laughed and ran the loofah down his legs and then nudged his hip so he would turn. She bit her lip and stared at his beautiful ass that begged for her to take a nip. "When is it my turn, mate, to wash every inch of your delicious body?"

Gen ran the loofah across his back and down to his ass. "When I'm done, you can have your turn." She pushed on him again so he could turn and rinse the soap off his back. She stared into his eyes and dropped to her knees. She lowered her lids and leaned forward to take his cock into her mouth.

He groaned and leaned back against the shower wall. Thankfully he was close enough he didn't pull out of her mouth. She ran her tongue around the tip of his cock, and then took him as deeply as she could.

Her left hand rolled his balls in her palm and her right maintained a tight grip on the base of his cock. She didn't want him coming to fast. Gen felt his hands dig into her hair and anchor her head for a moment, then he pulled her off his cock and to her feet. "Naughty girl, it's my turn to play."

Remy wrapped his arm around her waist and spun her so she was under the spray of warm water. She gasped as the water ran down her body. "Did I say naughty girl? I meant dirty girl. It's my duty as your mate to clean you up, starting with this nipple right here."

Remy bent down and sucked her nipple into his mouth. "I'll clean you with my tongue better than any shower could." Gen moaned and leaned her back against the wall. "Do your worst, but I think you missed a spot on my other breast."

Remy smirked at her and bent his head again. His right hand came up to tweak her other nipple and tug on it gently. When she moaned, he swirled his tongue and pinched her nipple at the same time. "Remy." Gen didn't say anything else but that single word. She heard his lion.

He continued to tweak her nipple with his fingers. "Ah, Gen. My tasty little mate. I can't get enough of you."

"God!"

"That's it my sweet mate. Let me show you how much I want you."

Her body throbbed from the recent orgasm and the fresh need for him.

Remy lifted his head and looked into her eyes. "Someone will come looking for us soon. I'm sorry, love. Tonight, I will take my time and worship your body as you deserve." Remy lined his cock up with her pussy and slid inside.

Gen wasn't sure who moaned louder, but Remy's golden eyes told her his lion was close to the surface. Remy slid out then slammed back into her, pumping his hips faster and harder each time.

"That's it, baby. Take my cock and suck it with your tight little pussy. Fuck, Gen. You're so tight. So hot."

"Remy, I'm coming, don't stop." Remy reached down and rubbed her clit with his right hand and wrapped her leg around his hip. "I'll never stop loving you." With his words, Gen yelled out and Remy slammed his hips into her one more time, grunting out his release.

Remy rested his forehead against hers and breathed for a moment. Having a mate was so much more than he ever expected. He let go of her leg, letting it drop to the shower floor. She could barely hold herself up. "This time we really wash up and get moving."

He laughed and stepped away, picking up the bottle of body wash. "I promise no foreplay, just washing your body. Next time, we take separate showers, or we will never get anywhere on time."

* * *

Twenty minutes later, Gen descended the stairs to see Remy pacing with a grin on his face. "Who gave you the catnip?" Remy turned and lifted an eyebrow at her. That shouldn't be sexy but everything he did made her wet.

Remy met her at the base of the stairs and held his arm out. "Allow me to accompany you to the party."

Gen's heart did a little pitter patter in her chest. God. Was she already emotionally attached to the lion? Oh, god. That was probably the dumbest move ever. She just met this guy. And even though she loved the idea of a fated mate, she knew better. Her heart argued that this was right. That he was her one. Logic smacked that down and yelled at her to keep it in her panties. She wasn't ready to be in love yet.

"Gen?" He asked pulling her out of her psychotic emotional battle.

"I would love that. Do we need to take anything with us?" She glanced into the kitchen to see if anything was laid out. She felt Remy giving her arm a slight tug as he walked to the front door.

"Bertha came by and grabbed some stuff. We were to hurry up and get our asses to the party already."

Gen was both entertained and embarrassed knowing Bertha was aware they were having sex upstairs. "Holy shit! What if she showed up earlier when we were in the kitchen?"

Remy let out a belly-shaking laugh, well, if he had a belly to shake at least. "Shifter hearing, remember? She would have known not to come in as soon as she got to the front door." Gen was sure her face was beet red. There was no way she wasn't blushing.

"How am I supposed to look anyone in the eye now?"

Remy chuckled at her again. "Let's find out." They turned the corner, and ahead, Gen saw everyone sitting around picnic tables and grabbing food from long tables set out around the area.

Remy dragged her forward when she tried not to move. "Remy, this is embarrassing!"

He stopped and stepped in front of her, tilting her chin up so they were eye to eye. "Shifters are not embarrassed by sex or the human body. You will get over it soon enough. Just enjoy the night."

Gen nodded and squared her shoulders. "Okay, let's go."

TWELVE

The closer they got to the tables; the more nervous Gen appeared. Out of the corner of his eye, he spotted Bertha with a big grin on her face. He subtly shook his head. The last thing he needed was her teasing Gen and scaring her off.

"Gen! Can you believe this place? It's so amazing! The food and the lions, I want to move here forever!" Leslie ran up with a huge smile on her face. He watched confusion move across Gen's face and he glanced around to see what else was happening. One of his men stared intently at the actress. He knew that look well.

He couldn't wait for Gen to discover Leslie's news. Things were taking a very interesting turn.

Remy listened to their conversation but

stayed a few steps away to watch and interact with his lions and the theater group. Mainly, he wanted to know what was being said about the present in Leslie's bed. News had to have traveled and everyone loved to gossip.

He noticed secret looks aimed at him from various pride members, but the side glances could be for him finding his mate. He wondered if someone said something earlier about keeping the incident quiet. With a sigh, he looked around for Gen. If the pride was going to ignore it for the moment, then he'd have to wait until they were off guard.

He frowned when he heard Gen gasp. "I don't understand. A few hours ago, you were ready to leave. What changed?" Remy watched Lane walk up behind Leslie. "Gen, meet Lane. He's one of the lion shifters and my mate!" Gen glanced at him and then back to the couple standing in front of her.

"Well, congratulations! I hope you are going to continue with the play then." Remy watched as others listened in on the conversation between Gen and Leslie. If the goal of the gutted animal was to get rid of Leslie, the plan backfired. Someone would do or say something to give themselves away, he hoped at least.

Remy moved around the gathering, watching everyone and chatting. He turned when he smelled a wolf getting close to their gathering. "Azai, about time you showed up. I was beginning to think you were ditching your friends for some alone time with your mate."

Remy turned and smiled at Dalissa. "Welcome, Dalissa, thank you for coming. There is someone I would like you to meet." Remy proudly walked over to stand next to Gen. "Excuse me, can I steal Gen away for a minute?" Remy didn't wait for anyone's response but wrapped his arm around her back and turned her gently to face Dalissa.

"Gen, love, I wanted to introduce you to Dalissa. She is mated to my neighbor Azai, who is the Whittip Pack wolf alpha. But Dalissa is a lion, so we like her best." Dalissa laughed and glanced over her shoulder at Azai who growled.

"Gen, it's very nice to meet you. Remy mentioned he would have some guests from a local theater group. I assume you are part of that?"

Remy stepped back and circled around Gen to reach Azai's side. "It's good of you to come over. I need your help with a small situation."

Azai smiled and looked around at the group of people. "Is this something we should discuss away from your pride?" Gen's laughter floated over to Remy and he couldn't stop the purr of contentment. "Congratulations, too, on finding your mate."

Remy glanced at Gen's beaming face. "Thanks, I wasn't ready but can't imagine anything else. As for what we were talking about, we can discuss it here. Keep an eye and ear out on the gathered guests. Someone doesn't want the leading lady to be on our land. I'm not sure if it's personal or pride related. The theater people don't know you, so they might talk freely around you."

Azai nodded and moved to Dalissa, whispering something in her ear then walked away. Dalissa stared after him for a moment and then turned back to Gen.

Remy heard her whisper, "I'm still learning earth culture. How about a trade? You help me out and I will teach you about lions, and not just earth ones." Remy turned his back so Gen wouldn't see him laughing. The shock on her face was enough to cause tears to run down his cheeks.

Finding out your new friend was an alien he was sure would be quite the interesting conversation piece. He listened for a minute more, then moved on to chat with his packmates and the theater members.

Bertha gave him the side eye, so he made his way to her. "Should I ask how many members of the pride will be finding their mates among our guests?" Remy cocked an eyebrow at Bertha and watched her for any reaction.

"You can ask, but I'm sure I wouldn't know the answer to that question."

Remy scowled at her. She had an innocent

smile on her face, and he knew she was full of bullshit. "Lane and Leslie are mates. Who else, Bertha?" Remy would be surprised if there were more mates in this group, but considering Leslie was a last-minute addition, there could be, by pure chance, one more pair to be found.

"It's not my place to share, now excuse me. I have to go stir up trouble." Bertha strolled away cackling, heads turning to follow her. He would love to know what the others really thought of her. Did they think she was as crazy as she pretended?

Out of the corner of his eye, he saw Ethan tap Star on the shoulder. He headed toward them to see how things were going. He chuckled when Star spun around and growled.

"Everything okay over here?" Remy asked.

Ethan's face was bone white and his hands shook. "I'm sorry. I didn't mean any harm. I just wanted to chat with you, ma'am." Remy smelled the fear coming off the man and he glared at Star.

"Oh, Ethan, I'm so sorry. I honestly didn't hear you approach behind me. I was distracted and just reacted."

Remy took a deep breath; nothing was wrong. Just a simple misunderstanding. "Star, everyone getting settled okay? Anything I need to know about?" Remy wanted to ask about the rabbit and if Star heard or saw anything since they left the cabin, but he wasn't sure how much

Ethan knew or if he should scare the man further.

"Everyone's doing fine. I'm sure you know Lane is over the moon happy. Bertha already spread the word she was going to throw a baby shower for them. Of course, you can imagine Leslie freaked for a minute. She asked if she was going to spontaneously get pregnant by mating him."

Star rolled her eyes and glanced at Ethan who stood staring at her. "Other than that, nothing new to report. I asked Jensen, Ryker, and Mitchell to patrol around the cabins and report anything suspicious."

Ethan bounced on his toes and Remy smirked at the man. He was clearly eager to share something with them. "I was wondering if you would accompany me to dinner one night, Star?" Remy took a step back to let Star handle his query and turned to walk around. He glanced at Gen to check on her and saw Bailey talking to her. The actress didn't look happy and was yelling at his mate. He stalked behind Bailey and listened in.

"Leslie is mated to a lion? What the fuck do you mean she isn't leaving now? She's planning to stay and continue the play?" Bailey didn't wait for Gen to reply but turned and stormed off into the surrounding woods, pulling her cell phone out as she went.

"Well, mate, that was quite the interesting

turn of events. Up until that point, were you having a good time?" Remy wanted her to say yes. He needed to know she was comfortable with his people.

THIRTEEN

Gen stared at Bailey's back as she walked away. She didn't know what to think about her outburst. So much had happened since she showed up at the potluck. She hadn't even gotten a chance to eat anything yet.

She shook her head and focused on Remy when she realized he asked her a question. "I'm sorry. I was distracted. What did you say?" Remy let loose a loud laugh and several heads turned in their direction.

"I asked if you were having a good time up until Bailey's little outburst." Remy wrapped his arm around her, and Gen couldn't stop the sigh of contentment she uttered.

"Yes, Dalissa is amazing, and why didn't you tell me there was a shifter planet?" Remy laughed when he heard her stomach growl. "Let's feed you and I will tell you what little I know about Aurora. Dalissa is really the best person to ask questions to, though."

Gen nodded and turned toward the tables filled with food. "So, I assume you know Leslie found her mate?" Gen glanced at Remy as they walked and saw him nodding. "She's planning to stay with the production, said she had us to thank for bringing them together so the least she could do was stay on and do her part."

Remy laughed. "Literally, her part."

Gen chuckled as she picked up a plate and started down the line of food. "Is there anything here I need to be warned about in advance?"

"Everything is as you would expect to find. I promise there aren't any surprises unless you want to take home some pudding and I can lick it off you later." Gen glanced at Remy waggling his eyebrows at her.

She burst into laughter and filled her plate with various types of food. "Don't worry. I'll be back for the pudding."

Remy pointed to a couple seats at a table on the outskirts of the area. "Let's sit over there." Gen led the way and saw Dalissa heading to meet them.

"Hey, Dali, grab some food and come sit with us. I would love to chat more!" Gen smiled at the man who followed closely behind her and turned to pull out a chair at the table. Once

Remy sat next to her, she started eating.

"So, Leslie has a lion mate, someone threatened her to leave, and my understudy is slightly angry at not getting her chance at the part. Whew, it's been a really eventful day. The only good thing so far is finding you."

Gen stared into Remy's eyes and couldn't look away. "Ah, very sweet, but I hope you count me as a good thing, too." Gen laughed and looked up at Dalissa.

"Yes, I am very thankful to have met you." She turned to the man standing behind Dali. "Azai, very nice to meet you officially. Please have a seat."

Gen continued munching on her food as everyone got settled. "Remy, I overheard some mutterings about the letter and rabbit left for the leading lady, but no one knew who was behind it."

Gen stared at Azai as he spoke to Remy, and then at Remy, waiting for him to explain what was going on. "Gen, I asked Azai to listen in on some conversations to see if he could figure anything out. Honestly, though, the only suspicious person here is Bailey. She was really upset when she stormed off. Do you think she would have anything to do with this?"

Gen contemplated Remy's words for a few minutes. "I haven't known her that long, just since we started staging. But I don't see how she could have snuck a rabbit into the cabin with no one knowing. Honestly, I can't see her catching and killing an animal. She might be behind it, but someone else had to help her." Gen turned to look at Dalissa. "This was supposed to be a simple learn about lions type of vacation. I never expected to deal with threatening notes, finding my mate, or anything like this." She laughed and shook her head.

Dalissa covered her hand and gave it a squeeze. "The best part of shifters is their loyalty. You are one of us now. We will help find out what is going on and protect you from anything that comes. You don't have to do this alone." She squeezed Gen's hand again and leaned back.

* * *

A few hours later, the party was wrapping up and Remy walked over with a container of pudding. "Bertha gave this to me. Said we looked like we would enjoy having some later."

Gen was positive she was blushing, and Remy's laughter didn't help at all. "Are you ready to head home?"

She grabbed the container from his hands and walked away. "Keep up. I have plans tonight and I'm not waiting all night on you." She laughed and listened to his footsteps as he rushed up behind her.

"You're not starting anything without me. When we get home, I am having my way with you. I have been thinking all night about spreading you out on my bed and licking pudding from every inch of your body."

Gen's core throbbed in time with her heartbeat. "I can smell your need already." Remy leaned close to her and took a deep breath.

Gen stopped walking when Remy swore under his breath. "What's wrong?" A moment later, she heard pounding footsteps coming from behind them. "Remy, one of the cubs is having trouble with a shift. We need you."

Gen gasped and looked at Remy to find out what needed to be done to help. "Don't worry, love. This happens on occasion. Go on home, and I'll meet you there shortly. This won't take long to fix." Remy leaned in and kissed her, then turned and walked away.

Gen's lips tingled, and she was thankful he wasn't watching. She was positive she had a dreamy look on her face. She sighed and started back to Remy's home. Every time he called it her home, she got tingles all over her body. Shifters loved so deeply and accepted their mates so fast. It was a bit hard to take in, but she wouldn't change it for anything.

She was so lost in thoughts and dreams of Remy, she didn't notice the rustling sound for a couple minutes. "Is someone there? Remy, is that you?" When no one responded and she didn't hear anything else, she kept walking.

"You shouldn't be here. No human belongs on this land. Leave or I will make you." Gen spun around, but no one was behind her.

"Come out where I can see you and tell me to leave." Gen craned her neck to see into the darkness that surrounded her. "Are you the one who left the animal and note for Leslie? Why are you doing this?" She spun in a circle again trying to place the sound of movement she heard in the woods.

She turned back toward Remy's cabin and started jogging. From behind her, she heard movement in the forest following her. Just before she reached the cabin door, she glanced behind her and saw a lion staring at her. He let out a loud roar and faded away from her eyes.

Gen raced into the cabin and slammed the door shut behind her. Her heart raced. Was the lion the one who told her to leave or a patroller who saw her on the path to the cabin? She needed to calm down.

Walking toward the kitchen, she remembered she carried the container of pudding. The front door opened behind her and she spun around, throwing her hand up to her throat.

FOURTEEN

Remy rubbed the cub's head and said his goodbyes. The poor thing had gotten frightened and shifted. Then he got scared that he didn't know how to undo it. Thankfully one word from him, the alpha, and the little boy was back to normal.

Remy laughed as he pictured the young face when he shifted and realized he was naked. Modesty was a funny thing and something most shifters outgrow quickly. He shook his head and opened the door to his cabin. His mind immediately thought about chocolate pudding and the fun to be had that night.

Gen stood in the kitchen and spun around when he walked in. When she threw her hand up to her throat and gasped, he realized he scared her. "Are you okay? What happened?" His lion pushed to get out and protect his mate. First, he had to comfort his mate, then he would find what scared her and end it.

"Walking home, someone followed me in the woods. They whispered, 'You shouldn't be here. No human belongs on this land, leave or I will make you.' I called out and got no other response. I even asked if they were the one who left Leslie the note and animal.

"I rushed here but heard movement around me the whole time. Just before I reached the door, I glanced back and saw a lion watching me. He roared and then disappeared." Remy quickly gathered her in his arms and rubbed her back. His lion wasn't happy, and he was pushing to get out and search for the threat.

Through the pack link, he contacted Bertha. *I need you to stay with Gen. Someone threatened her. I want to check out the area to see if anyone heard anything.* His heart raced at the thought of someone threatening his mate, his woman. She should be safe on his land.

"I asked Bertha to come over to sit with you while I check out the area and get with the sentries patrolling tonight." Remy stepped back and quickly shifted. He looked up at Gen to see her reaction to his lion.

She dropped to her knees and tentatively reached out. He waited for her to touch him or pull her hand back. When she did neither, he nudged her hand with his head. He hoped she got the hint it was okay to touch him. Hell, his lion was ready to roll onto his back and bare his belly for her. As long as she touched him.

He felt her hand gently stroke his mane and down his neck. When the door behind him opened, he turned and walked out. Bertha stared at him as he went by. She had her usual smirk on her face.

He almost felt bad leaving Gen to deal with her. He stopped outside the cabin and listened for the door shutting, then let out a loud roar. His pride needed to know he was out and something was amiss. Those who were on duty would come running if they were smart.

He waited impatiently for his enforcers to come to his side. Jensen was the first to arrive, then came Ryker, and Mitchell was the last to arrive. Through the pride link, Remy spoke. *Someone told Gen she and humans were not welcome on this land. The first threat was to Leslie and we assumed it had to do with the play and role she took on. Now, I think it's more. Spread out, search for any clue who threatened my mate. Circle by the cabins where our guests are staying through the night. We need to keep everyone safe.*

Remy watched everyone turn a different direction, and he went down the path his mate walked home. The only scents he found were from his pride. He expected that but hoped it would be easier to narrow down the suspect. He searched the area, checking in with his enforcers, but no one had any luck.

Remy padded back to his cabin and waited for Bertha to open the door for him to come inside. He could have shifted and opened it himself, but he wasn't sure if Gen was ready to see him naked in front of Bertha. Non-shifters were mostly prudes when it came to nudity and sex in general.

He padded through the door when Bertha opened it with a butler type impersonation "After you, milord." She cackled and walked out, letting the door slam behind her. Remy rolled his eyes and then shifted.

Gen stood from the kitchen table and stared at his naked body. "Well, that wasn't quite what I expected, but I love the view." She licked her lips and trailed her eyes up his body. He could feel his cock hardening with every visual caress.

"Keep looking at me like that, and I will bend you over the kitchen table." Remy growled when she licked her lips. Gen spun around and picked up the container sitting behind her.

"As good as that sounds, I'd prefer we put this to good use." Remy watched her saunter closer to him, swinging her hips. She ran her hand across his chest then climbed the stairs. "Are you coming up or are we christening your living room couch?"

She laughed and ran up the stairs, dropping

clothing on every other step. It took Remy a minute to follow, all the blood rushed from his head to his cock. He swayed slightly and his dick throbbed with every heartbeat. His mate was going to be the death of him.

He climbed the stairs and entered his bedroom. Remy's lion purred and pushed for him to take his mate and show her the true meaning of mate. He stalked to the bed and nudged her so she fell onto her stomach. "Don't move yet. I have been waiting to take a bite out of your delicious ass all night."

Remy climbed onto the bed and straddled her legs, his knees on either side of hers. He ran his hands up her thighs, across her ass, and up her back. Goosebumps broke out and she shivered with a light moan.

Leaning down, he licked her left cheek and massaged the right one. Gently he nipped the swell of her ass and then ran his tongue up to her lower back. "You taste as sweet as I remember. I wonder if the pudding will enhance or detract from your delicious flavor." Remy heard her breaths coming faster and she was shivering. "Are you excited, my love? I'm far from done, so relax and just feel."

He sat back on his feet and leaned to the side to grab the container of pudding on the nightstand. He thumbed off the lid and tossed it to the floor. "This might be a bit cold, but it won't last long."

He set the container next to her hip and dipped a finger in, lifting a generous helping and then rubbing it along her ass cheek, up across her lower back, and across her shoulders. She shivered as soon as the cold touched her skin.

Remy leaned down and blew across the cold pudding then ran his tongue along her body. Sucking up and nipping at her skin, he moved up her back. Gen moaned and lifted her ass to him. He bit down on her shoulder lightly. "When I make you my mate, I will bite you right here." He rocked his cock into her ass as he nuzzled her shoulder again. "Turn over. I want to lick chocolate off your breasts next."

FIFTEEN

Gen's whole body quivered at the husky demand in his voice. She flipped onto her back and stared into Remy's eyes. "Do I get a turn to play tonight?"

Remy's rich baritone laugh floated over her senses. "Not tonight, you don't. It's my turn to worship you. Now lie back and let me have my fun."

Gen couldn't imagine a more perfect mate. Every woman's fantasy was to be worshiped and that was what Remy was doing. She felt the bed dip as he sat back on his heels and dipped his hand into the pudding container, a wicked smile on his lips.

Over her stomach, his hand hovered, letting the pudding drip onto her belly, the cold making her jump. He moved his hand above her breasts and watched as more dropped onto her nipples. "Mmm, I can't wait to taste you." Her belly quivered and her thighs were covered in moisture. Gen gripped the towels under her body to keep from pulling Remy to her body. She needed him to do something, stop teasing her and touch her.

He leaned down and ran his hands through the pudding on her belly, smearing it over her hips, then up over each breast. He tugged on her chocolatey nipples and she felt them tighten in desire. He moved his hands up her neck and cupped her cheeks. Remy leaned down, tasting first one corner, working his way across her flawless lips. The flames that were always burning when Remy was anywhere near roared into a raging fire that only having him buried inside her could quench.

Her body vibrated with need as his hands roamed her chest. Needing to feel every inch of his amazing body rubbing hers, her hands flew across his body. Gen grumbled when Remy sat back on his heels and stared down at her.

Gently massaging up her well-toned legs, he paid special attention to the tops of her thighs. He teased along the edge of her pussy lips. She was soaked and eager to feel his cock slide between her lips.

Slipping his hands over her hips, he slowly licked her heated skin, following with soft kisses and the tip of his tongue. She squirmed on the bed, wanting him to hurry up but loving his slow torture. Remy moved down her body, lifting first one foot and then the other, kissing the tops of both her feet before beginning his journey back up her body to what enticed him the most.

The higher he climbed, the more Gen involuntarily tried to push her thighs together, but Remy was having none of it. Gently holding her legs where they were, he kissed the tops of her knees and then moved around to the backs. Trembling as he lavished her tender skin with his lips and tongue, Gen's fingers dove into his hair as she mewled, "Remy, I love you so very much."

Smiling against her skin, he hummed, "I love you more, Genevieve." She tried not to giggle, the sensation tickling her. Gen watched as he made his way to the tender flesh at the top of her thighs, her gaze drawn to his lust-soaked eyes. There was nothing like the effect he had on the one and only woman he would ever love. He grinned wickedly at the hitches in her breath and the way she moaned his name like her own sacred mantra.

Gen moaned again when he slipped his fingers between her thighs, the proof of her need flowing freely from her pussy. She was overwhelmed this time, just like every time, with the raw need only he could bring to live within her.

Sliding her legs farther apart, he licked the inside of one thigh and then the other, holding tightly as her muscles helplessly tried to close him out. He blew small puffs of air against the wet curls that covered her mound as just the tip of his finger teased her outer lips. Gen's nails scratched his scalp while she pulled his hair and whimpered, "Oh...oh, oh, Remy, please, please...you're...you're making..."

Evaporating in a wail of pleasure as he pushed first his middle and then his ring finger deep into the warmth of her desire, her body pulled his fingers farther into her depth. Working his fingers in and out, her juices flowed into his hand and down his arm. Gen thrashed her head thrash side to side, begging and crying out, as she panted, "Remy, please...please...I need you..."

SIXTEEN

L oving the sounds of her passion, he needed to wring every last ounce from her. Crooking his fingers in a come-hither motion, he teased and taunted the sensitive bundle of nerves deep inside her at the same time his thumb and forefinger gently squeezed her throbbing clit.

Screams of passion filled the room as Remy held Gen upright and continued working his fingers in and out of her. On and on, her climax continued, ebbing and flowing. It was the most miraculous sight he'd ever seen. Waiting as she floated back to earth, her succulent scent filling his every sense, the lion growled. "And now I shall have mine."

In one fluid motion, he put her legs over his

shoulders, placed his hands on her hips, and began to feast. Driving his tongue as far into his mate as he could go, Remy lavished the special bundle of nerves at the top of her channel with the tip of his tongue just as he had his fingers and held on tightly as Gen bore down on his face, rocking back and forth, driving his tongue even deeper.

Their rhythm was frantic. He tasted all of her, the warm sweetness of her arousal flowing down his throat. His lion roared. Nothing had ever felt so right, so wonderful, so complete in all of his life.

The walls of her vagina contracted over and over, faster and faster. Her juices dripped down his chin and onto his chest. He bathed in her scent as he drove his mate to completion, needing to feel her come into his mouth.

Howling as his frenzied tongue flew in and out of her, Gen's wails were unintelligible except for his name. Her hands were once again in his hair. With the force of her orgasm gaining momentum, he could feel her need to completely surrender just out of her grasp. Thrusting his tongue into her then immediately pulling it out, Remy gently bit down on her swollen nub and held on as she came with such force, it was a miracle they weren't both flat on the floor.

Not letting up, driving his tongue back into her again and again, he licked and sucked and teased, making her come over and over until she was begging, "Please...."

But there was none to be had. Remy needed his mate. He needed to be buried deep within her. Needed to feel her coming around his cock.

She gasped and whimpered.

Pulling his tongue out of her, he let her limp legs slide down his arms as he got to his knees. Marveling at the sight of his woman gasping for air and her bottom lip red from where she'd bitten it out of the sheer passion only he could give her, Remy could no longer wait.

Caught in her lust-filled gaze, he slowly pushed into her. Inch by glorious inch, closer and closer to being one with the love of his life, Remy panted as the need to lunge forward battled with the want to savor every single second of entering his mate.

"No, baby. I'm not having mercy on you. Not tonight. I'm taking. All of you. Every single inch of me will be deep inside you. Owning you. Letting your body know who you belong to. Me. Only me."

The tip of his erection bumped the mouth of her womb. Sighing in unison as her heavenly walls contracted around him, her body pulled him even deeper and held them together before she rolled her hips in the most erotic little figure eight that made his eyes roll back in his head.

The need to move became undeniable. Digging his fingers into Gen's soft flesh, he pounded in and out of her.

"Remy," she breathed his name out like a prayer.

"Yes, sweetheart. Tell me. Say it." He stroked deep and pulled back. "Tell me who you belong to."

"Fuck!" She choked out, raking her nails over his arms.

Lifting her hips, she met him thrust for thrust. Unbridled passion flowed between them. He couldn't go fast enough, couldn't get enough of her, needed to never leave the haven of his mate.

"Say it!" His growl thundered in the room at the same time he fucked her deep.

"You. You, Remy."

Leaning his much larger body over hers as they continued to move as one, Remy palmed both of her ample breasts. Loving the way they swayed in his hands as his body moved in and out of her, he massaged her supple skin with enough force to drive a squeal of pleasure from her lips.

Remy panted while trying to maintain control with his orgasm threatening to roll over and through him. Needing to climax at the same time as his mate, he tenderly pinched both of Gen's nipples between the thumb and forefinger of each hand then rolled his hips as he thrust in and out with unconstrained vigor. The change in position pushed the tip of his cock against the nerves at the top of her channel with every swipe while his hips pushed against her swollen and sensitive nub.

Screaming his name until she lost her voice, Gen's pleasure had Remy roaring against her skin and coming with such force, he had to let go of her beautiful breasts and slam his palms onto the bed to keep from collapsing onto her body. On and on, their combined ecstasy continued, wringing every drop of pleasure from them both.

Slowing his motions, softly moving with small strokes until both their heart rates returned to normal, Remy stayed buried deep within his mate. Wrapping one arm around her waist, he reluctantly let his still semi-erect cock slide from the sweetness of her pussy.

Rolling her over in his arms and laying her head on her pillow, he followed her down to the bed and pulled her close. Looking deep into her love-soaked eyes, he whispered, "I know you're human. I know you don't understand, but you will. I love you, Genevieve. You're mine."

A slow smile spread over her lips. "I don't understand it, but I don't care. I love you more, Remington."

* * *

The next morning, Remy woke with a smile on his face and reached out to pull her close, only to find the bed empty. He sat up quickly and listened for any sound in the house. When nothing was heard, he jumped out of bed, calling out to his pride.

Has anyone seen Gen? She's not in the house. Remy heard laughter first, then Star replied.

You lost your mate already. I think that's a record.

Remy sighed as more of his friends joined in and laughed at him. *I'm assuming she is fine since you all are joking instead of looking for her. Anyone care to share with me where she is, please?*

Remy climbed out of bed and walked into his bathroom to take a fast shower. He had a lot to do today, starting with checking in with Azai to see if he had any ideas what was going on around his land. He had a mate to bite and a group of actors to teach all about lions.

Relax, Remy, she's walking with Bailey. Nothing to worry about. She said you snored like a bear. Bertha's snort of laughter made the last part of her message muffled. Remy huffed and hurried through the shower. He was eager to get his meeting with the wolf alpha over then come back and kiss his mate.

SEVENTEEN

Gen tilted her head back and soaked in the morning sun on her face. Standing with Bailey at the head of the trail, she sighed. "This place is amazing. I can't imagine ever living anywhere else." She lowered her chin and smiled at the understudy.

Bailey snorted. "That mean you're not going to direct this play?"

Gen sighed for a different reason. "Let's walk for a bit, Bailey." Gen led them along the trail Remy told her went to wolf land and a stream. The morning was cool in the woods. Dew still covered many of the low-lying plants.

The unknown person who told her to leave was still out there, but she wasn't by herself, and it was the morning, broad daylight. Plus, she passed one of the enforcers on the way to the trailhead. They would be safe.

Gen wasn't sure how to start this conversation. In all her years of directing, she'd never had to discuss something like this.

"Why do you want to talk to me, Gen?" Bailey asked with impatience in her voice.

Agitated with the attitude, Gen stopped and planted her hands on her hips. "Spill it, Bailey. What's your problem lately? I'm beginning to think you are not good for the play. You're showing you're not a team player."

Bailey turned and stomped her foot. "You gave my part away to her." Bailey pointed toward the homes, so she assumed the actress was talking about Leslie. "She's not better than me. I know the part. I know the other actors. I know every inch of that stage, but you let her take what should have been my role!"

Gen's jaw dropped, her eyes growing wide. Bailey hadn't given any indication of her feelings when she announced they were auditioning for the part. Yeah, she tried out, but never seemed upset by not getting the part. What changed when they arrived here?

"Bailey, I'm so sorry! I knew you wanted the part, you auditioned for it, but not how much it meant to you. Why didn't you tell me?"

"Tell you? You haven't paid attention to anything since this Gerri Wilder told us to come here. That matchmaker screwed everything up and you just went along blindly. Don't worry. I will find her, and she will get what's coming to her next."

"Leave that woman alone. She has no part in this. She did us a favor. Yeah, Leslie and I found our mates, but that was a coincidence."

Bailey tossed her head and laughed. "Are you that fucking stupid? She sent you to this pride so you would meet your mate."

Her eyes narrowed. "How do you know that?"

Bailey stared at her for a moment. "I heard it through the grapevine like everything else. Including who got my part. You sure didn't tell me anything."

"You should have said something long before that, Bailey. We held a second audition. Why weren't you there?"

"I was going to, but somebody slashed a tire on my car. I couldn't get there. And by the time I got it towed and an Uber to the theater, you'd announced *she* had the part."

"Why didn't you call me?" Gen asked.

"I did," Bailey replied. "But it went straight to voicemail."

Gen hung her head. That was the message she'd accidentally erased that day after the auditions.

"I'm sorry, Bailey. That was my fault." A thought occurred to her. She couldn't believe she had to ask this. "Bailey, are you responsible for the dead rabbit and the note on the bed?"

Bailey turned her head and stomped along the trail. "No."

If that wasn't the most obvious lie she'd ever heard, and the woman was an actress. She would've thought a stage professional could pull off a false statement. Gen was correct that Bailey wasn't right for the starring role.

Gen set off after her. "Bailey, are you fucking serious?" She grabbed her upper arm and spun her around. "Did you —"

Too closely, a growl rumbled through the trees. They both froze. Gen thought there had to be a mistake. Then the answer occurred to her.

"Hi, there," she said, turning and talking to the trees. "I know we're on your land, but Azai and Dalissa, your alphas, know we're here and are okay with it. We're not trespassing."

The growling stopped and Gen let out a sigh of relief the said, "We'll just go back the way we came to the pride lands. Sorry to upset you." Gen stepped up the trail, dragging Bailey with her.

Snarling started in a different location. How many wolves were there? These were shifters, right? She should be able to reason with them. Then again, it was the forest, maybe wild wolves roamed the area, too. Shit.

"Bailey, how well do you climb trees?" Gen asked.

"W-what?"

"Trees, Bailey," Gen repeated. "Wolves don't climb trees."

"Oh, right."

Gen whispered, "Let's find you something to climb, and I'll go back and get help." The actress nodded. Surveying the trees nearby, Gen didn't see any low hanging limbs. These trees were old and tall.

Bailey pointed. "There. If you boost me up, I can stay there."

The tree was several yards off the trail, but it was the only one around. Gen nodded and they slowly made their way there. Gen twined her fingers together to make a step for Bailey to put her foot in.

As soon as Gen lifted the understudy, a huge-ass dog came out of nowhere, racing directly at her. Not a dog, but a wolf.

Panic ripped through her and she ran. Her heart beat so hard, it hurt. She had no idea where she was going. Her only goal was to not hit a tree in her mad dash.

Behind her, she heard a scream and turned. Bailey had fallen from the branch. The wolf slowed then headed toward an unmoving Bailey on the ground. She did the first thing that came to mind.

"Hey, doggie. Here," she jumped up and down, "Come get me. Hey!" The wolf looked over its shoulder at her. "Yeah, come get me, you piece of shit."

The wolf growled and lowered its head. Gen took off running again. As she expected, the wolf gained on her.

Through the trees, she saw a break where sun shined down on a cabin. What were the chances the front door was locked? Then she remembered they didn't secure their homes here. She changed her direction.

She wondered how the wolf hadn't caught her yet. Then she realized the wolf couldn't get much speed dodging trees and sticker bushes. Maybe she could make it to the home. She'd apologize to the shocked owner after she locked the front door.

With a leap she normally would've never attempted, she landed on the decking and stumbled into the siding. Her hand wrapped around the rusted door knob and pushed forward. The door flew open and she fell inside, somehow closing the door behind her.

She searched the room for a way to block the door. Then she noted the door had several deadbolts. That was contrary to what she knew, but hey, she wouldn't complain. When nobody came into the room to inquire what the hell was going on, she figured the owner was out.

Then she saw the cobwebs covering just about everything. Dust lay thick and untouched on all flat surfaces. No one had been here in a very long time.

In the open space where the kitchen and

living room were combined, she felt vulnerable. Her feet carried her into a bedroom where she pushed the dresser and bed against the door then crawled into the closet, closed the door and scrunched up in the corner.

She'd wait for someone to find her. Hopefully, before she died.

EIGHTEEN

Remy knocked on the alpha wolf's front door, ready to get this meeting moving. He had a mate to find and make love to again. There was still pudding leftover. A shudder ran through him, remembering last night.

The door opened to a lovely smiling face. Dalissa said, "Good morning, Remy." She breathed in loudly. "Whatever you were thinking about, share it with my mate. He's too stressed out." She winked and stepped back to let him enter.

He grinned and walked in, not knowing what to say to that. He wasn't the type to kiss and tell. "Uh, good morning to you, too, Dalissa. Nice to see you."

She laughed and closed the door. "Azai is in

his office." She pointed to a set of double doors made of thick mahogany. The wood didn't keep voices completely contained in the room, but if a shifter wasn't standing nearby, they wouldn't hear anything.

Remy pushed on the opened door and stepped in. His friend sat behind a desk as big as the wolf shifter was. The lighting was dim as there were no windows in the room. He would've preferred the natural light, but he understood the need for privacy in matters concerning the alpha.

"Come in," Azai said, waving him closer. "Have a seat." He gestured to the worn leather chairs in front of the desk. He had sat in these chairs many times ever since the two groups came to live side by side.

Remy's smile flipped upon hearing the wolf's tone. Whatever he had to say wasn't good. "Good or bad?" Remy asked.

Azai sighed. "Both, I guess." He lifted a glass and sipped. "Want a drink?"

He smirked. "I don't know. You tell me."

The wolf smiled. "Just water, for now."

He hadn't smelled alcohol, so he knew it was water, but it was fun to play along sometimes. "Whatcha got?"

Azai twiddled a pen in his fingers. "We haven't talked much since the incident with Megan, and that's my fault. I know —"

"Not really, Azai. I'm to blame, too. My

pride is suffering and I'm struggling to bring them out of their dark places."

Azai's head tilted up. "Yours, too?"

That surprised him. "What's going on with the pack?"

Sighing, the wolf alpha leaned back in his chair. "Everyone is on edge, easy to anger. Many are paranoid, can't sleep. Those who weren't taken don't talk to or trust those who were. Even the mates are having issues."

He wiped a hand down his face. "That's exactly what we're going through."

"Your typical PTSD symptoms," Azai commented. He agreed.

"What are you doing about it?" If something worked for the wolves, hopefully it would work for the pride.

"I'm seeing a PTSD specialist for advice," Azai said.

"How's it going?"

"Good, I guess. We're discussing ways for the pack to adapt."

"No," Remy said, "how are *you* doing?" He remembered the damage Megan had done to Azai. She had injected her *wombie* serum into him and commanded him to kill everyone in his pack. He would've if Dalissa hadn't reached him through their mating bond. If she hadn't been able to talk him down, Remy would have had no choice but to destroy the alpha wolf. He was glad it didn't come to that.

"I'm doing okay. I doubt my decisions more than an alpha should, but Dali says something if she doesn't agree. So far that hasn't been a big issue." Azai glanced at the door then leaned forward on the desk. "She also wants more sex." He snorted. "How many times have you heard the woman complaining about wanting more?"

Remy smiled. "Remind me to tell you a story about chocolate pudding later."

Azai's brow lifted. "Sounds interesting."

"Tastes great," he replied. "But first, what have you discovered?"

"Right," Azai stood and paced between the desk and wall shelves full of books. "The bad news is I wasn't aware how affected a few of the wolves are. Turner Lupin had been under Megan's control the longest. He's not the wolf he used to be. The good news is I don't think it has any effect on what's happening at your place."

"No?"

"Unless Megan herself came back from the dead, I don't see how any of this would touch the humans. No one in the pack has ever seen or heard of any of the actors. They're random non-shifters, yes?"

"Well," he answered, "random except for a couple being mates."

Azai nodded but said nothing. After a moment, he returned to his chair. "What has the owner of the houses decided? Are they selling or renting?"

The houses the wolf referred to were the ones where Megan held the wolves she'd captured and injected. Remy spoke with the owner and told him a story to cover the damages the interiors had taken — especially the dark stain on the floor where Megan's body bled out.

He'd been the one to take care of the corpse while Dali worked on finding the cure. He buried his beta on the edge of pride land so she wouldn't be disturbed either by strangers or pack members. That was all he was going to do for her after all she'd done to them and their friends.

"A couple of my enforcers cleared out all the chemicals and machines before we notified the owner. Luckily, he swallowed the story I spun without any questions. Last I heard, he planned to file with his insurance and put new flooring in and paint. Said it would take months to happen. After that, he intends to continue renting."

Azai nodded, again remaining quiet. A thought crossed his mind. Something someone had said the other night.

"Azai, I'm going to ask the theater group to put on an impromptu skit for us. Something to cheer up folks. How would your pack like to come over and watch?"

His friend smiled. "That would be great."

"Consider yourselves invited. I'll let you know where and when after I talk with my mate." He stood and they shook hands.

Azai led him out of the office and to the front door. "See you soon, lion boy."

Remy smiled at the tease. "Same, wolf man." As he turned, Dali came up behind Azai. Before the door closed, he heard her say, "I have an idea. I made chocolate pudding."

NINETEEN

Remy hurried home. He'd been at the alpha wolf's house for an hour and hoped his mate would be waiting for him. Ideally, naked in his bed. When he stepped inside his front door, disappointment flowed through him. He instantly knew she wasn't there.

Instead of contacting the pride, he'd wait patiently like a good mate should. He paced the living room, checking his watch every thirty seconds, not contacting everyone on the planet like a good mate should. He stood at the door, watching, not screaming at the top of his lungs like a—fuck it. He wasn't a good mate.

He opened the door to see Star climb the porch steps. "I came to tell you something is off with that Bailey girl. Before she left to meet with your mate, she was on her cell phone. Not that that is strange in itself, but she was far away from everyone and kept looking around like she was making sure no one was listening. I'm not sure she is dangerous, but just in case."

Remy walked off the porch. "Come on, let's find them. My lion won't rest until we see Gen and know she is okay."

Star walked behind him. "Should we put a call out to the pack to see if anyone knows exactly where they are? Or let them know we are looking for them?" Remy looked around the area, debating what to do. If he sounded an alarm, he might panic his people and they didn't need the stress right now.

Bertha, have you seen Gen or Bailey recently? I have a bad feeling and need to find them. Star nodded. "That was smart, boss. Bertha knows all the gossip. I have no idea how she knows it all, but she's smart!"

Remy glanced at Star in surprise. He hadn't realized she saw through Bertha's country bumpkin act.

Not since early this morning when Bailey was trying to hide her conversation on the phone. Would you like me to look around the actors' cabins?

Remy nodded at Star, who shifted and trotted down the trail that led to the cabins. *Yes, Bertha, I would appreciate it.*

Not far from his cabin, he saw Star talking to Jensen. His enforcer replied to her question.

"I passed Gen this morning on the trail from the alpha's home, said good morning."

"You didn't see Bailey with her?" Star asked.

He shook his head. "No. I wasn't sure where she was going. I figured she was meeting with her people. You know, to talk about whatever it is theater people talk about."

Remy joined them. "Bertha said Gen and Bailey were taking the trail to the creek."

"I haven't been down there since sunrise on normal patrol. Want to walk it now?" his enforcer asked. Remy was headed there before the question was finished.

Turning down the trailhead, he smelled Gen and Bailey had been there not too long ago. He followed the path and the scents passed the pride's land onto the wolves' property. They had to be at the creek still. He worried for nothing. But still...

When the scent vanished suddenly, he came to an abrupt stop. Nose in the air, he breathed deeply and stepped off the trail into the woods. He came to a tree where Bailey's scent left off and the ground cover was jostled like someone had been moving around.

"I don't understand," Star said. "Why does Bailey's smell stop here and Gen's goes on? Where is she?"

"Good question," Remy muttered and continued forward.

"A better question would be why did they leave the trail?" Jensen added. He agreed with that. The farther he went, the stronger her scent. A hint a fear tickled at his nose. His heart double-timed as did his need to find her.

He picked up speed, dodging trees and brush. "Gen!" She had to be close. Ahead, he saw the cabin that belonged to one of the wolves Megan had captured. He wondered if she was there.

Reaching the door, he pushed, but it didn't budge. Locked. Not what he expected, but since it was abandoned, he'd go with it. Star put her face against a window.

She said, "I don't see her, but her scent says she was out here."

His enforcer came from behind the small home. "I don't smell anything around the place. She must be inside."

Without delay, Remy threw his body against the door. He crashed through, landing on the floor among splintered wood. His animal picked up his mate's sent. Fear was heavy in the air. "Gen," he called out, climbing to his feet.

He heard commotion behind a closed door. "Remy! I'm in here." After forcing his way through that door, he finally held his mate in his arms. She sobbed and talked so fast, he couldn't make out what she was saying.

He shushed her and scooped her up, carrying her back to his cabin. Somewhere along the way, Jensen and Star left. It was only the two of them on his living room sofa. He held her tightly, waiting until her trembling stopped before asking any questions.

"What happened, my love? Why did you leave the trail?"

Gen wiped at her soaked cheeks. "A wolf chased us."

Rage tore through his veins. He would kill every one of those bastards — no. He took a deep breath, controlling his initial instincts to destroy the threat to his mate. First off, he hadn't smelled a wolf anywhere close to her path.

"A wolf? Are you sure?" he questioned.

She huffed and leaned away to give him a pissed-off look. "Of course, I'm sure."

He pulled her back to him. "Okay, relax." He rocked as he communicated with Jensen. *Did you smell a wolf in the woods?*

Not one recently in the area. It is the pack land, though, his enforcer replied.

Thank you.

Remy wondered what she'd actually seen. Everything had a scent. Even scent blocker had a smell. If there wasn't a smell, there wasn't an animal.

Gen jerked away from him. "Oh my god. Is Bailey all right? I can't believe I forgot about her."

"What do you mean?"

"Bailey. Didn't you find her?"

He read panic in her eyes. "I'm sure she's fine. Can you tell me what happened in words I can understand?" He grinned to show her he was teasing. He sat quietly as Gen told him her story.

He remembered the tree where the actress's perfume lingered. There had been no sign of her in the woods. She must've made her way back to the cabins they stayed in. But why hadn't she sought help for Gen? He telepathically asked Star to check the visitors' lodges for the woman. She replied quickly that Bailey wasn't there and nobody had seen her recently.

Gen snorted. "Of course, she's not there. She's the one who put the rabbit on Leslie's bed."

"Are you sure?" he asked.

"Pretty sure. When I asked if she had anything to do with it, she flat out lied. I bet she left. Got back to her car and went home to hide." Gen chewed her bottom lip. "Shit. Now I need to find another understudy for the lead."

Remy hugged his mate to chest. "Don't worry about that. We'll figure it out."

"At least the threat is gone. I need to tell Leslie everything is fine now." She sighed and melted in him. He wanted to take her upstairs and ravage her body to take her mind off what happened, but another thought crossed his mind.

"I wanted to ask you something," he said.

"Sure. What?"

"Do you think your group could put on a short skit for the lions and wolves to watch? Something comical to make them laugh and take away their worries for a bit."

"We didn't bring anything with us..." When she quieted, he wondered if she was okay.

She pulled away from him with a huge smile on her face. "I know exactly what I want to do." She jumped to her feet and paced a moment. "I need to talk with Bertha. She can tell me what I need to know."

With that, she ran out the front door calling back to him, "Don't worry. I got this. See you later."

He chuckled. He was thrilled to see the twinkle back in her eyes. She was in her element, doing what she loved — directing. With his mate once again safe, he had other things to check on.

First, he had Jensen go to the parking area to see if both vehicles the troupe brought were there. The enforcer reported that only the car was there. So Bailey had taken off without getting help for Gen. If he ever saw that woman again, the confrontation wouldn't be pretty.

Next he wanted to talk with Azai about the wolf Gen spoke about. He paused before calling the alpha. The fact there was no proof of a wolf worried him. He didn't want to accuse them if the claim was false. But he believed Gen had seen something.

He stepped outside for a bit of fresh air. In the distance, he heard a lot of commotion. Remy hurried to the center of the village and found what seemed to be controlled chaos.

His people—men, women, and cubs—ran here and there, some carrying baskets, the men carrying power tools. Was that a chainsaw? What the hell?

Dalissa jogged up a path that stretched between the pack and pride and stopped beside him. "Got here as fast as I could."

Remy glanced at her. "Why? What's going on?"

A wide smile grew on her face. "You'll have to wait to find out, I guess."

Across the way, he saw his mate waving her arm in the air. "Dali, over here." The female alpha wolf giggled at him and ran to join his mate.

Oh, shit. This couldn't be good.

TWENTY

A couple hours later, Remy sat on the wolf alpha's front porch, watching the goings on in the wolf town center. After Dali had been with Gen for a few minutes earlier on pride land, everyone started carrying things to the wolves' side.

Now, the wolf community center building was abuzz with activity, literally. The chainsaw he noticed earlier had made its way over here. Hammers pounded away while sheets and sheets of plywood were carried in.

The women and children ran between a few houses and a dress shop, carrying tan bolts of material. One time, a pup crossed the street wearing a brown hoodie with what looked like ears sewn on top of the hood.

The biggest thing Remy noticed was how happy everyone looked. They smiled and talked excitedly when passing on the sidewalk — wolf and lion. Didn't seem to matter what species, they all got along.

"So," Remy said as he gazed upon the hustle and bustle, "you don't have a clue what's going on either?"

Azai rocked in his chair, spring water in hand. "Nope. My mate told me to plant my cute ass in this chair and to not get up unless to go inside the house."

Remy sipped his drink. "Yup. I got the same thing. Except my ass is gorgeous, according to my mate."

Azai rolled his eyes. "TMI, cat."

Remy laughed. Azai crossed an ankle over his knee. "What I find amazing is the sudden change in morale, energy, and community. Even those who haven't come out of their homes in weeks are moving about. Whatever your mate has planned has helped my people already."

"Can't blame my mate alone," Remy said. "Yours seems to be directing traffic just as much as mine is."

When noon rolled around, men carried over picnic tables and set them out front of the community building. Dishes filled with salads and leftovers from potluck night appeared along with lunch meat and bread. Sandwiches were prepared and passed out as workers walked by.

Occasionally, Gen stuck her head out of the dress shop or the community center and blew him a kiss. His heart lit up every time he saw her shining face. His animal wanted to join in the fun and sneak its mate away for a quickie behind a building, but he didn't want to get an ass chewing for disobeying by getting up.

After eating, Remy broached the subject he'd been thinking on for a bit. "Azai, this morning, Gen said she was chased by a wolf when she was walking the trail to the stream."

The alpha stiffened, liquid in his glass sloshing over the side. "One of my wolves?"

"Are there others that aren't yours?" That was news for Remy.

"There are the wolves that are native to the area. Non-shifters."

"I haven't seen any wild ones," he said.

Azai laughed. "Of course, you haven't. They're smart enough to know when someone higher on the food chain is in front of them."

His statement reminded him too much of Megan's philosophy. But he knew his friend didn't mean anything by it.

Azai said, "I guess she's okay, seeing that she's stirred up a hornet's nest in your pride and my pack."

"Yeah. This project is right up her alley, taking her mind off the incident. The thing is I didn't smell a wolf or any other animal where she was."

Azai glanced at him. "How can that be?"

Remy shrugged. "Also turns out that one of the actresses is responsible for the dead rabbit and threats."

"Their own people?" the wolf asked. "One of them caught, gutted, and left a carcass without anyone seeing them? A female at that?"

Put that way, it did sound a little farfetched. But Gen was adamant that Bailey was the culprit. Maybe he'd revisit this with her later when she'd had some time to reanalyze what happened.

Azai sat quietly rocking. Too quietly. Remy asked, "What's going through that head of yours?"

His friend kept his gaze forward. "The only time I've experienced an animal not having a scent is when Megan used her chemical scent blocker."

Remy startled. He thought back to the trees where Megan started her rampage. They couldn't figure out who had carved the messages into the bark because there was no smell to identify the perpetrator. The reason was a spray Megan created that blocked all scent except for a minute chemical smell only Dalissa could detect.

"Do you believe in ghosts?" Azai asked.

"I don't want to," he replied.

A young boy cautiously approached the alphas on the porch. Azai lifted his hand. "Hello, Chauncy, how are you today?"

"I'm good, Alpha Azai." The pup stood with wide eyes staring between the men. Remy thought about the cub who needed help shifting. When he walked into the home where the child lived, the boy became speechless. Remy guessed the cub thought he was in trouble. After commanding the little lion to retreat completely, giving control back to the boy, they ate popsicles and colored a picture of a giraffe together.

He couldn't wait to have cubs of his own. He hadn't discussed this with Gen yet. She'd probably freak out seeing that they had been together a couple days.

"So, Chauncy," Azai finally said as the boy hadn't moved, "what brings you to my door?"

The small arms lifted slowly, revealing a cell phone in his tiny hands. "I was sent to get a picture of you."

"You were, were you?" The pup nodded slowly. Azai sat forward in the rocking chair. "Well, come on up here and take your photo, son."

The boy grabbed onto the vertical post of the railing since he couldn't reach the top. Shoot, he couldn't have been more than four years old. When he finally made it onto the porch, and had the phone lifted, Azai crossed his eyes and stuck out his tongue. The phone clicked and the boy giggled.

The child swiveled toward him. "You, too, Alpha Wemy." Before Remy realized the boy was aiming the phone at him, the device clicked and the pup scurried off the porch. He could only guess what his expression had been.

"Who do you think sent him?" Remy asked. He almost didn't want to know. If it was Dali or Gen, that couldn't be a good thing. "And why send someone so young?"

Azai rocked back and laughed. "Any one much older than him wouldn't know how to work the damn thing." The men laughed.

After a few more hours of watching dozens of wolves and lions going in and out of the main building, Remy became anxious, wanting to hold his mate. And just like that, her beautiful face appeared next to the porch. He held a hand out to her and she slid to him, snuggling into his lap.

"How are you men doing?" she asked. "You've both been very good by staying here, letting Dali and me work."

"And why is it we have to stay here while you ladies have all the fun?" Remy asked.

Gen smiled. "Because we need someone to pick on and you two alphas won the draw."

Azai leaned toward them. "Those are the scariest words I've ever heard coming from a female."

Gen giggled then kissed Remy. "The show will begin soon."

His jaw dropped. "You've put together a play in one morning and afternoon?"

She grinned. "Well, sorta."

"Does this play have a title?" Azai asked.

"Yes," Gen said, hopping off Remy's lap and stepping onto the grass. "I call it the *Lion King, the Condensed Version*." With that, she ran toward the main building, laughing as she went.

"No," Remy said, "those are the scariest words ever from an alpha mate."

TWENTY-ONE

The pack community center was a warehouse-sized building with enough space to hold the entire pack for celebrations and gatherings. It also housed a full stage with overhead lights, speakers, and curtains. No wonder Dali brought everyone over here. This would almost be like a real play.

He stood at the back of the room with Azai and Bertha. With both groups, the place was standing room only. He thought everyone except those patrolling the land were here.

He surveyed the room and noticed something he'd not thought about. When attending shifter functions with multiple species or more than one pride, each division gathered among themselves. All the Babcock pride sat together or all the bears claimed one area for themselves, rarely integrating.

But here, lions and wolves, male and female, mates and singles, young and old, mixed into one combined force. They talked with those around them and laughed and shook hands.

Azai leaned sideways toward him. "Have you noticed —"

"Yup," Remy said, not needing his friend to finish his words. He knew exactly what a fellow alpha would pay attention to: his people.

Azai continued. "I can't believe these are the same people who were here yesterday. I don't know how your mate did it, but she just pulled off a miracle."

His chest puffed up, proud of what his woman had done. Bertha slapped his arm. "Just wait 'til the end of this, then tell me what you think." Then she did something that scared the living shit out Remy — Bertha giggled.

He would've run if the lights hadn't dimmed at that moment. The curtains opened to a white screen hanging down. A heart thrumming drum beat rose in the silence. He glanced at the side of the stage and saw one of the men operating a CD player that piped in music. He assumed the song playing was from the original soundtrack someone had.

No need to worry about copyright infringement. He was sure this makeshift skit created in one day wouldn't become a Broadway hit.

Behind the screen center stage, a bright light shined forward, throwing the shadow of a person dressed in loose-fitting garb with feathers and headdress onto the screen. The light's low angle made the shadow ten feet tall.

The music swayed and the image with it, slow and sinuous. The beat vibrated through the floor and into his body, waking a primal awareness that flowed in his veins from the time of his ancestors.

The shadow raised her arms at her sides. "From the day we arrive on the planet, and blinking step into the sun..." The voice of Lane's mate rang clear and true through the cavernous space. Her voice and the music combined into a soul-lifting feeling he'd never experienced before. His lion was enraptured.

Too soon, the song was over and the screen lifted to reveal the back wall painted in a jungle theme. Along the side, slender trees stood with oversized leaves draping from the trunks. If he had to guess, he'd say the scene was set in a forest.

A spotlight turned on and his mate stood brilliantly on the far side atop a rock-looking prop. A soft beige cloak hung over her shoulders down to her bare feet. Around her delicate neck, a rainbow of beads showered her chest. In one of her hands, she leaned on a tall walking stick, and the other, she held out toward the audience.

"Welcome guests of young and old, feline and canine. Tonight, we present to you the coming-of-age story of a cub destined to be king but determined not to. Before we begin, the gods have asked me to bestow this information upon you. Though this story is based on a real-life play, we have taken creative liberties to adapt it for our use."

Remy mumbled to himself, "What does that mean?"

Bertha whispered, "It means she changed alotta shit."

"Fantastic," he muttered.

The light on his mate dimmed and the center stage lit revealing a plethora of different ages in tan pajama jumpsuits with lion ears on their heads and tails out their behinds. The audience oohed and ahhed at the sight. They all ran around without rhyme or reason, so it seemed.

Heavy drum music played in the background as his mate's voice came through the speakers again. "Times in the jungle had been prosperous. Trees grew lush for many years. Waters flowed deeply year 'round. And the pride had ample food for everyone. They are blessed more for the next great king has been born! Simba!"

Those on stage parted like the splitting of

the Red Sea, and an infant in a beige onesie sat in the center. Where the child's face would've been was instead a two-foot-tall cutout of Remy's face with a pacifier photoshopped in his mouth.

The audience roared with laughter. Gen had to wait for the hullabaloo to quiet down before she could continue.

Remy had wondered what his expression was when the pup had taken his picture earlier. Now he knew and it wasn't pretty. He looked like a drunk hobo. Yeah, he hadn't shaved this morning. Nor brushed his hair apparently.

Remy feigned anger toward Bertha. "Why didn't you tell me I looked so godawful." He ran his fingers through his hair.

Bertha smiled. "Because that's what we're used to."

Remy rolled his eyes as Azai laughed. Remy wondered what Gen saw in him. Thank goodness the mating pull was so strong.

Gen continued with the narrative introducing Scar. The audience booed and hissed at the bad guy. He jumped around and batted at the smaller dressed lions on the stage as they ran from him and hid.

Gen leaned forward and pointed her stick at the audience. "Then the worst comes to pass. The pride is betrayed by one they trusted."

Remy felt a sudden tension in the room the word *betrayed* created. All the problems both groups had suffered from Megan came back to mind. Today had been the first time the weight of reality had lifted. Now it hung front and center again.

When he looked at the stage next, his super-sized face was attached to a boy about the age of ten in a lion suit.

"Of course, Simba wasn't alone," Gen recited. "With him was Timon. . ." Dali skipped out in yellowish coveralls and ears attached to a headband. The audience cheered.

"What is she?" Remy asked Bertha.

"A meerkat."

"What's a meerkat?" he asked.

"Dali is a meerkat."

He rolled his eyes. "That's not what I meant," he said. She shushed and told him watch.

"And Pumbaa, the warthog..." his mate said. The next character came onto the stage walking backward so they only saw the back end of the hog. "And we all know what issue Pumbaa had."

At the same time, those on stage and the audience made a fart sound. The warthog's tail shook in time with the sound effect. Remy wondered why the character hadn't turned around yet.

After yet another flatulent sound, the actor spun around and the audience howled with laughter. This character had a two-foot-size cutout of Azai's face with eyes crossed and tongue out. Now he understood what his mate said when they needed someone to pick on.

His friend groaned and dropped his head into his hands. Remy hadn't laughed so hard in years. Gen's giggle echoed over the speaker.

"Hakuna matata," Gen said.

The three on stage repeated, "Hakuna matata."

"It means no worries for the rest of your days," she said. Remy watched as the three on stage ran around, laughing like kids. Including both his and Azai's big heads.

"But who really lives in a world with no concerns?" Gen went on. "We want that for our children, but what kind of adult does that bring into the world?"

If he hadn't been paying attention, he would've missed the passing of his own cutout from the ten-year-old to a male teenager. He danced with Timon and Pumbaa, playing tag and laughing.

"One not ready for the challenges to come. Difficulties are a part of life Simba doesn't learn how to cope with. He has no role models to watch while growing up."

Once again, the image of his face was handed off to a male adult and the three settled to the stage floor lounging without a care in the world. In a matter of a minute, he'd watched himself grow from a cub into an adult. But

Simba wasn't ready to face what came next.

The lights lowered and actors rushed off stage. Another screen lowered, but this one was in front of the jungle set. When the lights came up, the stage had transformed from a lush, colorful image into a brown, dead world. Several lions, including Scar, lazed around.

His mate's voice rang in his head, sweet and soothing. "With Simba gone, Scar became king." Boos and hisses erupted from the peanut gallery. Scar swiped at the audience like he could reach them, then settled back into his comfy position.

"With no love and care, the jungle slowly died. The rains dried up and the food moved on to more fertile ground. They were on the edge of extinction."

On stage, a female approached Scar. Gen narrated. "They told the evil king there was no food to be found. The streams had long ago turned to dust. He had destroyed the beauty and resources that once were in abundance. They were starving to death."

Scar rose and pretended to backhand the lioness. She landed with the other lionesses catching her. Growls erupted, vibrating the floor similar to how the drums had.

Gen's body stiffened and he read the fear in her eyes. He pulled away from the wall to go to her, his lion wanting to protect her, to tell her everything would be all right. But Bertha laid a hand on his arm, staying him.

Gen blinked and her shoulders relaxed. Her glance shot to him and he smiled and winked at her. That was his girl. Bold and strong in a room full of predators who could eat her in two bites. His mate.

Gen cleared her throat and continued. "Only one person could save them from such disaster, the rightful king. But where was Simba? He had been gone for so long." Centerstage dimmed and a small section to the front side lit. His two-foot-tall adult face sat with a female about the same age.

Bertha leaned over. "That's Nala," she said, "Simba's friend and mate." He nodded and understood what was happening. "Now pay attention," she chastised as Gen spoke.

"Simba was afraid to return to the pride. His best friend didn't get it. Nala wondered why Simba didn't want to make things better. What was he afraid of?"

Gen stepped down from the rock she'd stood on the entire production until then. Walking stick in one hand, she went down on one knee.

Another, older, lioness gracefully floated into the spotlight around the two. The pride audience members gasped and bowed in their seats. Remy felt the blood drain from his face as he stared at the regal woman. He hadn't seen his mother since his father died. How had they contacted her? Gotten her here so quickly?

The previous alphas were beloved by all in the pride. When his father passed, his mother had gone into seclusion away from the pride. He saw her rarely. It was hard for a mate to survive without their other half. Most took their own lives soon after. He was told the living mate felt like their soul had been torn in half.

"My son," the queen said to the characters at her feet, "the time has come for you to make your stand and take your rightful place as heir to your father." Her eyes raised and locked onto his. "I know the pain you all suffer. It is impossible to understand why others do what they do. It is not our duty to understand, but to instigate healing.

"Hakuna matata can only last so long. You have your mate to help guide you with the pride. Your father and I prepared you the best we could to face life's challenges. Now you must meet them head on.

"A Scar runs deep; he will always be there, waiting for a weakened moment, trying to drag you down. You must not let him destroy what you have built. Cherish your natural resources." The queen glanced at Gen bowed on a knee. "You must fight to save them all."

Remy's mother lifted her arms to encompass the entire audience, making contact with individual members of both pride and pack.

"The past is behind you. Leave it there. Learn from your mistakes, vowing to not repeat them. Why do you allow the actions of another to rule who you are?" She paused as if waiting for an answer. None was given.

"Yes, you were betrayed in the worst way, but the price has been paid in flesh. Find it in yourself to move on. If not for yourself, then for the sake of the children. Do not make them suffer the sins of others."

Her arms lowered and she set her fists on her hips. "Now, every one of you put on your big boy/big girl pants and snap out of this funk before I get the notion to tell you all how it's going to be."

She lowered her head and the light faded out. Then she was gone.

Silence engulfed the room. Each person had just been handed their ass by his mother. Something he had no clue how to fix, she accomplished in five minutes for both species. Tough love. *Love* being the key word.

The play finished quickly after that. What more was there to say? His genius mate had provided the vehicle to save his people. Now the question was did it work?

The characters came back on stage when the closing song started. They joined hands as Lane's mate walked centerstage with the beautiful exotic outfit the shadow did no justice to.

Leslie sang, "Can you feel the love tonight?"

Remy fixed his eyes on his beautiful mate on stage. Yes, he felt the love. Love that would surpass any obstacle thrown in their way. It was time he showed her how much he cared. Tonight.

Bertha hit his arm and nodded toward the audience. Every person held the hand of their neighbor: black, white, tan, gray, whatever. Together, they would pull out of this grief and bring each other up from the depths they had all wallowed in for too long.

He felt the love.

TWENTY-TWO

Gen's heart squeezed when Remy hugged his mother. Bertha had spoken to the old alpha recently to get advice on how to help the pride heal from their ordeal. So when Bertha called again this morning and told her the plan, Mrs. Leandros chartered a plane and flew in. It wasn't hard to sneak her in since everyone had been so busy and Remy was sequestered on the porch.

Gen served Mrs. Leandros tea in Remy's kitchen after the large gathering for dinner. Joining forces, the men set up tables and chairs for everyone who wanted to attend. Many of the women cooked and baked during the day, knowing there would probably be a feast afterward. And they were right. When was a shifter not hungry?

"Genevieve," Mrs. Leandros said, "the play was fabulous. You are an amazing director. And to pull all that together in under a day..."

Remy wrapped his arm around her and dragged her onto his lap. Gen glanced at his mother and blushed. "Remy," she whispered, "not in front of your mom."

Mrs. Leandros laughed. "You have a lot to learn about being a shifter mate, my dear. If my son had waited any longer to haul you close to him, I would've taken him aside and scolded him."

"Mom," Remy rolled his eyes, "I'm not a cub anymore."

Gen giggled at his reaction to his mother's loving care. The woman was amazing and Gen could only hope to be half as strong as the alpha mate was.

"Mrs. Leandros," Gen said, "please call me Gen. I'm so thankful that you decided to participate in our play."

The older woman set her cup on the table. "I'd prefer you call me Nana since that's what my grandcubs will call me." Her serious eyes drilled into Gen's. "You have started working on that detail, yes?"

Gen felt herself pale. She wasn't about to admit to her mate's mother that she was having sex with her son. Oh my freaking god, no.

Nana's eyes crinkled at the edges and her

lips curved up. "I'm just teasing you. Sorta. I do want grandcubs, but I'll give you a few weeks."

"Moooom," Remy whined. "Stop already."

She waved a hand through the air, dismissing his complaining. "Of course, the play wasn't the only reason I came. I wanted to meet my son's new mate." She glanced at her son. "And I must admit, he has been blessed with a good one." She winked at Gen.

"Nana," Gen said, "did you do any acting when you were younger? Your stage presence is remarkable. With your first word, the audience was eating out of your hand. And your soliloquy was simply brilliant."

Nana smiled modestly. "No, child. My experience comes from real life as do my words." Her smile faded a bit. "You two have a rough road ahead if the pride continues with these ridiculous doldrums. I hope I've provided enough of an alpha command to snap them out of their PTSD."

Gen couldn't believe what she just heard. "PTSD? The whole pride? How?"

Remy rubbed her back. "It's a long story I'll tell you another time."

Nana's eyes widened. "You don't know what happened?" Gen shook her head. "But I thought the purpose of the play was to show them what they were suffering from and what would happen if they didn't heal."

"I didn't have that in mind when I wrote it,"

Gen replied. "I just wanted to add as much humor as I could. People around here need to laugh more."

"I agree," Remy's mother said. "Well, this proves to me that you are going to be an excellent female alpha. Your subconscious picked up on the problem and worked to come up with a solution which came out in this play. Everything you said in a roundabout way is what a psychiatrist would suggest."

Remy kissed her cheek. "That's my girl."

Nana rose with an empty tea cup in hand. "I'm turning in for the night. I've had a long day." She set the cup in the sink. "I'll see you in the morning." She stopped in the kitchen entrance and turned to them. "Please don't worry about waking me tonight. I do want those grandcubs."

Gen wanted to fall through a hole and have the world swallow her. She'd never been so embarrassed in her life.

Remy nuzzled her neck. "You heard her. Let's go make grandcubs."

Her jaw dropped. "Never in a million years would I have sex while your mother is in the next room. Are you insane?"

He frowned. "Oh come on—"

"No. Not gonna do it. I don't think I can. I'd be freaking out the entire time."

Her mate sighed and hugged her. "All right. Tonight we sleep only. But after my mother leaves, I'm banging your brains out."

She grinned. "I will be ready to be brainless. Let's go to bed. I'm exhausted."

He slid an arm under her knees and lifted her. "Then to bed we shall go, director fabuloso."

TWENTY-THREE

The next morning after breakfast, Gen dragged her ass, and her mate's gorgeous one, to pack land to help strike the set. So many helped in putting it together based on her weak description, the least she could do was assist in taking it down.

On their way in, Azai snagged Remy for a quick meeting in his office. The wolf alpha looked concerned, but he held his shoulders back farther than yesterday. In fact, she noticed the same camaraderie in folks as there was yesterday when they had all come together to accomplish a shared goal.

Several were outdoors in the sunshine weeding flower beds in need of a manicure and mowing lawns that had gone uncared for.

Everyone waved and called her by name. Well, everyone knew who she was and if they disapproved of her being the alpha's mate, they had plenty of opportunity to let her know.

Inside the community center, scores of people rambled around. Some were dismantling the wooden structure supporting the jungle scene while others served food to those on stage.

Dali hugged her tightly. "Thank you for helping," she told Gen.

She laughed. "It's my fault it's here. I should *direct* it being taken down, no?"

Her friend winked. "You are the director." Dali handed her a flathead screwdriver and guided her toward the trees to pry out the heavy-duty staples attaching the paper leaves.

"How was the evening with Mrs. Leandros?" Dali asked.

Gen blew out a breath. "I've never been so nervous in my life. Even before a major opening night. I was lucky I didn't spill hot tea on her."

"When is she leaving to go back home?"

Gen rolled her eyes. "Probably not until she's sure she's got grandbabies on the way."

Dali leaned back and laughed. Yeah, it was funny—this morning. No so much last night.

One of the ladies called out to her and Dali, waving a good morning. "You know," Dali said, "that's been happening all morning."

"What?"

"Happy people spreading joy."

"What do you mean?" Gen asked.

Dali frowned and scooted closer to her. "My arrival here wasn't the best of times. I became mixed up in the plot Megan dreamed up to rule the world."

Gen didn't want to pry into the details, but she was dying to know what the hell happened. Judging by Remy's reaction when the event was mentioned, it had to be something devastating.

Dali continued. "Since I've been a part of the pack, they've been trying to overcome the ordeal. Several of our wolves were deeply affected." She studied the men working onstage for a moment. "But today feels like a new day. Like the past has been laid aside and the focus is on the present. I think you've saved our pack."

"You can thank Remy's mother for that. She's an incredibly powerful alpha with a heart of gold. I can learn a lot from her." Maybe she should ask Nana to stay a while and help her become a good leader.

"Gen, you've already mastered how to lead a group. How long have you dealt with divas and prima donnas in the acting profession? It can't be easy working with so many personalities and making them mesh."

Gen snorted. "You got that right. Some people think they are God So and So. They hate when I remind them they breathe the same air as everyone else."

The two gathered the wood and carried it out the rear loading dock to the chipper where a stack of wood had been started.

"Excuse me," a voice came from the side of the building. Gen glanced over to see a scraggly looking man, too thin. "Are you Genevieve?"

Gen started to step toward the man to shake his hand, but Dali grabbed her wrist, gently keeping her in place.

Dali smiled. "Turner, where have you been? We've been worried about you."

If Gen hadn't known Dali so well, she wouldn't have noticed the change in her friend's voice. A different tone used when talking to someone skittish. Turner dragged the toe of his shoe in the gravel.

"I-I've been helping a friend," he said.

"Do what?" Dali prodded.

Turner stuffed his hands in his pockets and glanced over his shoulder. "Just helping them. Genevieve, Jensen needs to talk with you. He has some information about Bailey."

Oh shit. Bailey hadn't even crossed her mind. She'd been so busy with the play. She should call her to make sure she was all right, even though the woman had done a horrible thing to someone who was not competition. First, she should hear what Jensen had found.

"Thank you for letting me know, Turner. I'll be there in an hour or two," Gen replied.

Turner gasped. "No. You have to come now. It's important. She needs you." His hands wrung, one over the other, and he glanced over his shoulder again.

Well, shit. Guess she'd go see what was wrong. Gen pulled out of Dali's hold. "It's okay," she told her, "I'll be back shortly."

Turner turned and walked away. Gen turned to Dali. "Stay here. If it's an emergency, I'll send Turner back so you can get more help."

Dali didn't appear happy, but Gen shouldn't delay if Bailey planned on doing something else. Or if she really did need help. She followed Turner to pride land and a small cabin. He opened the door and walked in, leaving her outside.

Okay.

She stepped inside, looking around. "Hello? Bailey?"

The home was cozy in a sparse way. Only a couple pieces of furniture graced the living area and the kitchen counters had nothing setting out. No feminine touches. Was this Jensen's place?

For some reason, she thought she was meeting him outside on the trail since that's the only place she'd seen him. He hadn't helped with the play, but he was an enforcer with important responsibilities.

She heard a crash in an adjacent room.

"Stupid motherfucker. That's not what I

told you to do." Turner flew out of a room and crash landed in the living room. Was that the enforcer's voice? She hurried to Turner. He looked to be unconscious but breathing steadily. She slid a blanket off the sofa and balled it under his head.

"Turner?" When he didn't respond, she approached the room Turner came from. Jensen was bent over a counter, breathing heavily. She felt the rage radiating from him. Her eyes studied the shelves and strange equipment sitting on tables. She didn't know the names or uses of the machines, but she recognized a lot of stuff as scientific in nature.

One shelf held several white containers with the universal symbol for poison on them. Sulfuric acid, formaldehyde, chloroform, calcium cyanide. A spray bottle had the words "no smell" written on it in black marker.

Oh, fuck. This probably wasn't a good place to be right at that moment. She took a step back but Jensen's gaze snapped up, pinning her to the spot.

Fuck. Fuck. Fuck. What to do? She could act like she hadn't seen him toss Turner like a throw pillow into the other room. That wouldn't work. While she debated, a growl emanated from Jensen, growing louder by the second.

She took another step back. "Uh, I should get back."

Jensen shook his head. Oh, shit.

She wondered what she could say to remove the anger in his features. He was a freaking shifter. The last thing she wanted was him angry and taking it out on her. She needed to distract him. "We need to get a doctor over here for Turner right now." He glanced over his shoulder at her.

Gen froze mid-step.

His bloodshot eyes looked wild, almost scary. "He will be fine. Shifters heal themselves. Give him a minute."

Her pulse doubled, instinctual fight or flight kicking in. Sensing her reaction to him, he turned away. "Sorry, Gen," he said. "I've been up all night. I'm a little testy, I guess."

She swallowed hard, scared shitless, but trying to stay calm. "What have you been doing? What's all this stuff?"

The enforcer stepped back and looked around. "This belonged to a dear friend of mine. After she was murdered, I kept her things. It's all I have left of her." His voice cracked.

This woman sounded like someone he loved. "Why were you up all night?" she asked.

He stared at her with narrowed eyes, then his shoulders relaxed and he sighed. "I'm trying to figure out what I should do. I'm torn on which way to go in a decision."

Glancing back at Turner, still wanting to call a doctor, she asked herself what would Nana do? WWND. She'd offer an ear without getting all up in his business then give advice. Now the issue was what did she say to help him?

Next to her sat the bottle with "no smell" written on it. "What's this for?" she asked, stalling for time. It seemed out of place unless he was cleaning the room.

He smirked. "That's something my friend created. You spray it on something and its scent is destroyed."

"Destroyed?" She'd never heard about smell being *destroyed*. Covered, yes.

He nodded. "I don't know how the chemicals work, but if you sprayed it all over you, not even a shifter would be able to detect you were there."

A shudder worked through her. Sounded nefarious. Why would one want to destroy their scent for a benevolent reason?

"Cool," she said, playing it calmly.

"Have any advice for me, Alpha?" His tone was off. This wasn't the Jensen she met.

"Well, when I'm not sure what to do, I weigh the pros and cons and decide if I can live with the consequences of each option. Then I make a decision and don't look back."

Jensen smiled and pulled a bottle from a table, then grabbed a washcloth from a stack of linens. "I like your answer, Alpha. I think you'll do well here." He poured liquid from the container onto the cloth. She needed distance from him. Without making it obvious. Besides, she was truly worried for Turner. She slowly walked back into the other room. Turner was still unconscious on the floor. She then remembered why she was there.

"Bailey," she said, staring at the prone male. "What have you found out? Is she planning on trying another stunt?"

"How about I take you to her?" he said directly behind her. Startled at his closeness, she immediately tried to move away. He was faster. He lifted the cloth still in his hand and smashed it over her face. The chemical she breathed in made her cough then her world faded to black.

TWENTY-FOUR

Remy wanted to be no place else on earth than where he was right now—arm around his mate, his pride around him, and the sunshine and fresh air surrounding them all. Life couldn't get any better and he planned on having many more days like this one.

Last night was a bit of a downer because his mate was too shy to have sex with his mother in the guestroom, but he'd live with that. For one night. Any more than that and he'd take her downstairs into the kitchen and eat her to his heart's content, guests or not.

Just the thought of licking and sucking her juices from her core made his cock fill. Shit. He wondered if they could find a nook or cranny somewhere on the wolf land where they could have a quickie. Damn, he was hard up and wanted to taste her.

He would've loved to stay in bed, but his mate was too kind-hearted and wanted to help the wolves any way she could. She was the best and she was his.

When he saw a scowling Azai heading up the sidewalk, he had a feeling fun time was over. The wolf alpha greeted his mate with a good morning and shook his hand. "I hate to do this," Azai said, "but I need to steal your mate for a bit."

Gen beamed at him and kissed his cheek. Her sneaky hand slid around his back and squeezed his ass. Guess he wasn't the only one ready for lovemaking.

"You can have him," she said. "I don't need to be distracted while I'm trying to work." She winked and continued to the community center building.

Azai walked him down the sidewalk. "I see mate life is suiting you well."

He chuckled. "I thought I wasn't ready, but Gen showed me I was overdue. She's not only wonderful with me, but the whole pride. I can't believe the change she's made in the lions in such a short time."

"You can trust Mother Nature to bring you what you need when you need it."

Remy smiled. "If you mean Mother Nature being Gerri Wilder, then you'd be correct." Both men laughed. "What do you want to talk about?"

Azai casually looked around. "Only in the office where additional ears won't accidentally overhear."

Remy blew out a breath. This couldn't be good. He noticed a lot of wolves were out and about this morning. A nice change from the empty streets and parks that had been the norm for too long. And surprisingly, he saw a lot of his pride here mingling. It was just a matter of time, he guessed, to forge lasting friendships.

After closing the office doors, Azai gestured for him to have a seat and instead of sitting behind the desk, his friend sat beside him.

"First," the wolf alpha said, "I want you to know how much I appreciate all that Gen, your mother, and the pride did for us yesterday. I believe we are now on the path to healing and becoming the united pack we used to be. The show was quite the experience."

Remy nodded. "I feel it had the same effect on the pride. Mother knows best they say."

"She certainly does." Azai rested his elbows on the arms of the chair. "Perhaps she would give me advice on how to handle one of my pack."

Remy's brow raised. "I can ask. What's up?"

"The other day we were talking about the pack that had taken an especially hard hit from

Megan."

"Yes, I remember that conversation," Remy replied.

"Then you'll recall the name Turner Lupin."

Remy nodded. "He's the lone wolf with the cabin down by the stream."

"Also the first of Megan's victims," Azai added.

Remy's heart crushed with that knowledge. That bitch had ruined so many lives. And he never saw it coming.

"Remy," Azai said, "it's okay. People like Megan, you can do nothing to help. They hide what they're doing so well, sometimes they don't even know what they're doing. It's a mental thing you can't see, smell, or touch."

Remy knew he was right, but that still didn't take away the guilt.

"Anyway," Azai said, "that's not what I wanted to talk about. It seems Turner has been missing for the past few days."

"Missing?" Remy asked.

"He's not been at the facility where he should be and nobody has seen him. Normally, I wouldn't give a second thought about one of my wolves taking a hiatus from the world. But when you mentioned Gen had been chased by a wolf and you didn't smell anything, only one thought came to mind. But you told me you had your men clean out the house."

Remy nodded. "A few of my enforcers did.

Took out the equipment and all the shit she had amassed."

"Do you remember Megan talking about the chemical spray that took away an animal's scent?"

"Not sure if I heard about it from you or her, but I know what it does. Isn't your mate the only one who can detect the chemical solution?"

Azai nodded. "Don't take this the wrong way, Remy, my friend, but are you sure your men destroyed everything Megan had?"

He opened his mouth to say emphatically yes, then closed it. He hadn't seen what the men had done with everything firsthand. He was too busy dealing with the rest of the fallout. He closed his eyes and called out to Ryker.

What did you and the others do with Megan's things from the house? How did you dispose of it?

Jensen said he would take care of everything and we took it all to his place.

What did he do with it?

There was a pause to the reply. *I don't know. I assume he carted it all into the city to properly get rid of it. That's what I would've done.*

Thank you, Ryker.

Next, he contacted Jensen, but he got no reply. Only two reasons for that — he was dead or refusing to answer. A bad vibe carried over the psychic connection with his enforcer. Something that made his wolf sit up and take notice. Something was wrong. Remy thought back through the past days to see if he missed some aspect concerning Jensen. He'd have to check on it later. Right now, they were dealing with Azai's wolf.

"What is it?" Azai asked. Of course, another alpha would pick up on the vibe.

"One of my enforcers isn't replying to me."

Azai's brows raised. "Should we check on him?"

Remy shook his head. "No. I'm more concerned with your wolf and his whereabouts when my mate was on the trail yesterday."

Footsteps approached the office doors. Dali stuck her head in, about to say something, then her mouth snapped closed and her forehead crinkled in confusion.

"What are you doing here?" she asked Remy.

"Talking to your mate," he replied. He turned to the wolf. "Are we in trouble and shouldn't be consorting?"

Azai frowned. "If we are, nobody told me."

Dali huffed and strode inside. Sweat soaked her shirt and wet hair was tucked behind her ear. "Stop being so ridiculous, you nincompoops." She turned to her mate. "Guess who I saw a little bit ago."

"Sally from the shop," he said.

"Well, obviously, her. I went there this morning."

"Mac," he answered.

She cocked her hip. "He's the mailman. Of course, I've seen him." She shook her head. "You know, never mind."

Azai winked at Remy.

Remy had always envied how the two wolf alphas got along so well. Not only did they love each other, they liked each other. Maybe not at this moment, though.

Dali leaned toward her mate. "Turner Lupin."

"Really?" Azai glanced at him. "How was he doing?"

"He seemed more strange than normal. Very agitated and always looking over his shoulder."

"What was he doing?" the wolf asked.

"He told Gen that Jensen wanted to see her. Something about Bailey."

He was out of his chair before Dali finished the sentence. Too many questions concerning the same group of people circled in his mind. If his mate was involved, he wasn't waiting any longer.

He ran from the alpha's home to Jensen's cabin in record time. Azai and Dali followed. He threw open the door, stepping in and taking a deep breath. Jensen and his mate had been there recently. He also smelled a wolf.

"Oh my god," Dali shouted and rushed into the living space. She knelt beside a man he recognized, barely. She shook the man's

164

shoulder. "Turner, wake up. Turner."

That was the zombie man he saw standing next to Megan? Holy shit. He looked deathly ill. Dalissa seemed to have a handle on it so he investigated the rest of the home. The room he entered answered his questions to Ryker.

Everything from Megan's home was in this room, including her concoctions and syringes. Fuck. Why was Jensen holding on to all this?

"Remy, look." Azai picked up a bottle with the cap off. Chloroform.

Fear shot through him, nearly sending him to his knees. Had Jensen kidnapped his mate? Why would he do such a thing?

"Hey, guys..." Star's voice came from the other room. She must've seen them running and joined in. "Check this out." They hurried over to find her pointing at a spray bottle on the floor next to a wadded-up cloth. "There's chloroform and Gen's scent on the rag." She rolled the bottle with her shoe. The words "no smell" were revealed.

"Son of a bitch," Remy roared, shaking the walls. He burst out the front door, sniffing for the direction his mate went. Only her scent entering the cabin existed. He must've sprayed them both with that shit before leaving. There was no way he could trail them.

Fury so intense ripped through him that his lion took control. He shifted and looked for something or someone to kill. The only movement his lion saw was his mother hurrying toward him. His lion backed down immediately, especially when seeing the look on her face. Shit. He felt like a cub again.

"Remington Allen Leandros," she said as he cringed. "That better not have been an uncontrolled shift. We taught you better than that."

"But, Mom, he has my mate."

"Who has your mate?" she asked.

"Alpha Leandros," Star said, "if you'd come inside, we'll fill you in." The group gathered in the small room with the scientific equipment and each took a turn telling their part in Megan's story.

After they were quiet, Remy said, "I just don't know why he would take her. She hasn't been here long enough to even do anything to him."

"Which means," his mother said, "it has to do with something before she arrived."

Remy pulled at his hair. "I have no idea what. He was fine."

She said, "I suggest you track them to see where they are and confront him."

"That's what's the most aggravating," Remy growled. "We can't smell either of them."

"I can," Dali said.

Remy wanted to kick himself. Of course, Dali could. They were talking about it in the office before she came in.

Dali stepped out of the room, pulling her shirt up. When Remy reached the door, one of the largest lionesses he'd ever seen trotted by. Bertha was big, but Dali was huge. Azai was one lucky bastard.

Nana stepped back. "Let me know how it turns out. I'll take care of Turner. Sounds like he's injured beyond what his wolf can fix."

"Thank you, Mrs. Leandros," Azai said. Dali lifted a paw to say her thanks.

Remy gave his mother a nod and turned to the alien lion shifter. They followed Dali as she led them through familiar territory. They passed the trees that had been etched by Megan and through the field to the road and across.

Remy stopped. "Is this going where I think it's going?" he asked.

Dali nodded.

"Fuck me," he muttered and continued without needing Dali. She hung back and shifted, Azai handing her clothes over.

Star caught up with him. "Where are we going, Alpha?"

"To the house where Megan had her lab and held our wolves hostage."

She gasped. "Fuck me, indeed."

TWENTY-FIVE

Gen woke with the worst headache she'd ever had. She opened her eyes and the room spun. She groaned, trying to swallow the bile rising in her throat.

"Good timing, alpha mate. He should be here soon. If he was smart enough to figure it out."

Peeking under one eyelid, Gen didn't recognize where she was. It looked like an empty house someone had moved out of recently. Needed paint badly. She couldn't see much else. The windows were covered with heavy material. Jensen stepped into her view.

Gen tried to move where she was seated and realized she was bound to the chair. "What the fuck, Jensen? What are you doing?"

Anger radiated from his eyes. "Doing the same thing to my alpha's mate as my alpha did to my mate."

Her head was still spinning too much to think that hard. "What?"

He slapped her face, snapping away the sleepies that remained. She worked her jaw up and down. "Hope you enjoyed that because Remy won't be happy when he hears about it." Her senses where coming online. She recalled being knocked out at Jensen's cabin. He must've carried her here. They couldn't be too far from pride land.

"Remy won't be happy about a lot of things. And rightly he shouldn't for what he did to my mate."

"What did he do?" she asked.

He grabbed her chin, digging his fingers into her gums. "He murdered her, that's what he did. In cold blood."

"Why would he do that? It doesn't sound like something he'd do."

"Shut up, bitch. You weren't here. You didn't see what he did to her."

"Oh, so you're going to kill me now so two people are dead. That's smart."

He boxed her in the head, sending searing pain down her neck. "I said shut up."

She watched as he shook a bottle with milky contents. He poured a vial full then grabbed a syringe from a box. Panic swept through Gen.

She hated shots, doubly so when they held questionable contents. He laid it on the table.

From the same box, he pulled out thick pillar candles, set them on the floor and lit them. She could see better, but there wasn't much to see.

"Jensen," she asked, "were you at the play?"

"No," he said, "I was on patrol. Heard it was quite the moving experience. The old alpha mate using her 'persuasion' abilities to kick the pride into gear."

"What do you mean by *persuasion*?" Gen asked.

"You're not a shifter so you wouldn't understand."

"Try me," she taunted.

"Alphas are alphas for a reason. The have an inherited power to make others bend to their wishes."

"Even if you didn't want to do it?"

"Yes."

"So, Remy can walk in here and make you let me go?" she said with a bit of smugness.

Jensen laughed hysterically. "Do you think Megan or I are that dumb?"

She didn't know this Megan, but it sounded like the wheel was spinning but the hamster done died. "I suppose not," she replied.

"Smart girl," he retorted. "Megan created a serum that allows a shifter to not be affected by an alpha's power."

"Really? How's that work?" Before he answered, another voice came from behind a door. Was that Bailey?

"Shut up, bitch!" Jensen yelled. "You'll get yours."

"Why are you holding her? I thought she ran away because we knew she was the one who put the rabbit on Leslie's bed."

Jensen snorted. "That woman can't do shit by herself. I put the damn animal on the bed for her."

"Why would you do that? I don't get it."

"That was before I knew you were the alpha's mate."

"Ah, then you hatched the plan to kill me in revenge."

Bailey kept yelling, her high-pitched voice was hell on her headache. After a few minutes of the noise, Jensen stomped across the room and through the door to where the actress was.

"I said shut up!"

Gen heard a slap and the squealing stopped. Then she heard Bailey's sobs.

"You said you loved me, that I was your mate," the actress said between heaves of air.

"You really thought I loved you? Humans aren't fit to be mated to shifters. We are superior in all ways. You were simply a means to an end. You walked in and I could tell right away you were pissed about something. It only took a few nice words and you spilled everything. You were so easy to manipulate, it's kinda sad really. You just proved Megan and my theories about humans. Waste of space. Lions are the superior species."

He walked back into the living room. "In fact, I don't need you anymore." He picked up the syringe he'd filled earlier. "Might as well make sure the shit still works." An evil smile spread across his face as he headed back to Bailey. "Hold still, love. This will only hurt for a second."

Oh shit. He was going to inject her understudy with the same poison he would be giving her. She yanked on her arms, but they were bound tightly to the chair. But her legs were free.

With Jensen's back to her as he went into the other room, Gen got to her feet, bent in an awkward position, and charged him. Her shoes were quiet on the floor. Luck was on her side that she favored rubber-soled shoes to dress shoes.

Jensen stepped into the other room and raised the shot in his hand, trying to be dramatic or stupid, she didn't know. She lowered her head and plowed into his back as hard as she could. A sharp pain zipped down her spine, but she felt everything—everything—when she crashed to the ground, so she hadn't damaged her spinal cord.

After shaking the walls with a roar, Jensen picked himself up off the floor, grabbed the syringe, and lifted it over his head, ready to ram it into her body.

She couldn't move one inch with the chair strapping her down. This was it. She was going to die. Shitty part was she didn't get to say goodbye to the only man she'd ever loved.

TWENTY-SIX

Stepping through the kitchen door, memories flooded Remy's mind. He and Dali at the table, watching the spectrometer do its thing. He was clueless the whole time of what Dali was attempting, but it had worked.

In the next room was the blood stain on the floor where Megan's body, a lump of bloody flesh actually, had lain. A shiver ran through him, but it was time to let it go, to let the past remain there and move on.

Suddenly, the house shook, a crack running up a wall, onto the ceiling. They stumbled through the archway into a large empty space. A box lay on the floor with several lit candles spread around.

A door was open where a scream came

from. Remy ran straight in without stopping to assess the situation. His shifter-fast reflexes had him grabbing an arm swinging down with a needle in hand. He tackled the male body, slamming them both into the wall, crushing a huge area of faux-wood paneling.

Delivering punch after punch to his enforcer's face, Remy's lion wanted to kill the man for touching his mate. Azai wrapped his arms around him and pulled him away. Remy fought to get back to the bastard. He was still breathing.

"Remy!" The alpha wolf's power washed over him, not strong enough to command him, but enough for him to get control over himself. Azai set him on his feet.

"Thanks, man." Remy lunged toward his mate on the floor. He popped out a claw and sliced through the ropes. Gathering her in his arms, he checked her over quickly. Once he assured himself and his lion she was safe, he pushed her behind him.

"Star watch over them and take them to my cabin. I will be there shortly." Remy moved forward and glanced at Bailey. She wasn't worth his time, but she had to be punished. "Azai, don't let this one get away. We can deal with her later." Behind him, he heard Star roar and Bailey started shaking.

Star and Dali helped the ladies out of the room while Azai carried the chair into the other space. Remy grabbed his ex-enforcer by the scruff and dragged him out, throwing him into the chair his mate was tied to.

Both alphas stood staring at Jensen slumped in the seat.

Azai asked, "Want me to hang around or you got this?"

"Nah," Remy answered, "watch over the mates. Ask Bertha to take care of the actress. She knows what we do."

"Got it." The wolf walked out, leaving him alone with his man.

"Jensen, I have to say I'm shocked. I never saw this coming. Why now? I don't understand how you could betray our pride like this." Remy moved closer to the man as he spoke.

"My family, you killed my family."

Remy froze, trying to understand what Jensen referred to. "I never killed anyone."

Jensen snorted, and Remy saw fur sprouting on his arms. "Megan?"

Remy was confused now. Jensen wasn't related to her or mated to her.

"Megan wasn't my mate according to the fates, but we both believed it to be true. She was my everything and you took her away. First, from the pack, then from my life. I bided my time until your mate came along."

How had he not noticed an affair between his one-time beta and enforcer? "Why would you keep your relationship with Megan from me? To what purpose?"

"You're soft, Alpha. You're not fit to run a pride the way it should be. You're a human lover. You were on your way out. Megan was a much better leader than you'd ever be."

Okay. That was news to him. How about some turnaround play?

Remy said, "Do you know exactly how Megan died?"

"You killed her, you bastard." He started to rise from the chair, but Remy shoved his shoulder down.

"I didn't touch one hair on her head, Jensen. She did it to herself. She injected Dali's alien blood into herself thinking she would gain the same strength. Dali's blood is poison to a human body.

"No," Jensen growled, "she wouldn't do that without me. We were to do it at the same time."

"She never once brought up your name. She had no intention of sharing any power with you. She wanted it all and that's what killed her, by her own hand."

"That's a lie! She loved me. I loved her. I saw you bury her body. She was nothing but ground up meat. You did it to her."

This time Jensen sprang from the chair, hate fueling his body and need for revenge. He slammed into Remy and they rolled across the floor, knocking the candles over, scattering them.

Jensen wrapped his hands around Remy's throat. "I will kill you. I will kill you."

The alpha jammed his knee into the enforcer's stomach, taking his breath away as well as his hands. Remy scooted back, gulping down air.

"Look, Jensen. We can move past this—"

"I will never forgive you for taking her from me." He dove for Remy and they rolled again, closer to the kitchen. Remy didn't want to hurt one of his pride, now that his mate was safe. He was raised to love and care for each one. Never, and they meant never, kill a fellow lion.

Jensen slammed an elbow into the side of his temple. His head spun, making him off balance. His enforcer used the opportunity to smash a fist into his face a couple times before Remy threw him off. His eye started swelling, narrowing his vision.

At the moment, his brain registered smoke in the air. The entire far end of the room was ablaze. Shit, how had that happened? This had gone far enough. He pulled his ace card—his alpha ability.

"Jensen," he said, power running through his voice, "back down now."

The man laughed and swung a partially shifted paw at him. The blade-sharp talons barely missed him. "Jensen, stand down."

The man smiled and shifted into his lion.

How was he able to ignore the alpha command? Remy shifted also. The floor creaked from their weight. Was there a basement or cellar in this house? Floor joists and two-by-fours couldn't hold the weight of two adult shifter lions. He retreated farther into the room. The intense heat of the flames burned his backside.

Change of plan. He needed to be closer to the kitchen, away from the fire. Chunks of flaming wood dropped from the ceiling where holes had been burned through. Fuck. The ceiling joists had a slight bow to them. They wouldn't remain up much longer. They had to get out.

Jensen, we need to leave, he said through their mental connection. His fur felt like it was a piece of toast left in too long.

You are not going anywhere, Alpha. You must pay for what you've done. His enforcer paced side to side as if a line was drawn and he was dared to cross it.

Jensen, I did not kill Megan. Her greed was her downfall. She wanted to rule the whole damn planet.

She would've succeeded.

No, she wouldn't have. A true leader rules with their heart. Megan had no heart.

Jensen roared. *That's not true. She loved me,* he said as his cat leapt at Remy.

Even though Remy was a large alpha, he was nimble and quick. He dodged to the side, but Jensen's claws stretched out and raked down his ribs and hindquarters. Remy landed on his feet, like cats always do, but the touchdown wasn't as graceful as usual. His big body slammed against the wall, bringing down a chunk of ceiling. The wood creaked and groaned. It was all coming down.

His focus turned to getting away, then Jensen crashed onto the floor...and sank. The weak support material gave way and his enforcer fell from his sight, along with half the room.

Shit. Remy shifted and crawled toward the hole. The cinder-saturated air burned his lungs with every breath, but he wasn't about to leave one of his own.

Leaning his head over the chasm, he saw Jensen's lion lying on its side, small fires burning around him like he was the center of a sacrifice.

"Jensen," Remy yelled and immediately coughed, "shift and we'll get out of here!" He stretched his arm over the side. The height of the basement below was only seven or eight feet, but the size of the opening allowed him to only get so close.

When the lion didn't reply he moved around, trying to get nearer. Then he saw why there was no answer. A piece of wood, mostly hidden under his furry mane, had pierced Jensen's neck and stuck out the other side. A dark stain grew quickly around his head.

Go, Alpha. Save yourself. The "voice" in Remy's head was weak and raspy.

No, not without you. My job is to keep my pride safe. That includes you, right now.

Let me go, Alpha. Let me be with my mate. My lion has gone insane without her. I can't control it anymore. I miss her too much. Even though she was crazy, I still love her.

Yes, true love trumped everything.

Apologize to Turner for me. Tell him I never wanted to hurt him. Dali knows where the cure is.

You can show me when we get back. Now shift and heal yourself. A loud crack came from overhead and an inferno rushed toward him. He pushed away then curled into a ball to protect his head from being crushed.

After a moment of no movement, he kicked and shoved insulation and singed wood piled on top of him. Crawling out, he coughed and kept low to the ground. He turned toward the hole, still determined to save his friend, but the gap wasn't there; it had been filled in with ceiling and roof debris and burned exceedingly hot.

He tossed a broken board aside. He'd dig if he had to. Then he felt something wrap around his ankle

"Don't be a dumbass, Leandros," he heard Azai's voice. "He's gone. Get out of here."

He hesitated. What if —

"And the fire department is on the way.

They don't want to see your bare ass."

He was naked from his shift earlier. Remy hated to admit defeat, but fire cleansed and returned ashes to ashes. Maybe this was for the best.

May you and your mate find each other again. Goodbye, Jensen.

TWENTY-SEVEN

"Star, let me out of here! I need to know he's okay. I can't stand the not knowing." Gen paced the kitchen, glancing at the front door every few minutes. "I'm sorry, hun, but Remy told me to bring you here and keep you safe. That's what I'm going to do. You are my sole responsibility right now."

The front door opened and Gen spun around with a relieved smile, but Bertha walked in. "Don't look so down; you're going to give me a complex. Do I smell?"

Gen's smile flopped and she sighed. "I'm happy to see you, Bertha. What did you do with Bailey?"

Bertha smiled and walked into the kitchen, dropping into a seat at the table. "I called a friend of mine in the human sheriff department. He put her in the county jail and lost the paperwork. Figured it would give us some time to decide what to do with her."

Gen didn't know how to respond, so she shook her head and kept pacing. Star interrupted her thoughts when she patted her on the back and left the cabin. "Where is she going, Bertha?"

Bertha smiled and pushed a chair out from under the table. "I asked her to go. I want to talk to you about the mate bite and what to expect. I assumed Remy hadn't had the chance to tell you what to expect or how it worked. Am I right?" Gen didn't know what to say but she was sure her cheeks were bright red.

"Um."

Bertha waived her words away. "Do I need to start with the birds and the bees, or I guess in this case, lions and humans?" Gen choked on the spit in her mouth and gaped at Bertha. "You good? Okay, I will move on then." Gen hoped Bertha was pulling her leg and not serious right now, but she suspected she was going to have the talk whether she wanted to or not.

"Fine. I was just kidding. Oh, not about the mate bite but the sex talk. Shifter hearing is good, so I know you two are compatible in that department." Gen was sure her face was on fire now. She could feel the heat in her cheeks.

"I don't even know what to say right now."

"No worries, you just listen to Aunt Bertha, and I will take care of everything else."

* * *

Twenty minutes later, the front door opened again and Gen practically shot out of her chair. She was ready to be rescued by anyone at this point. If Bertha made one more reference to Remy's *stinger*, she might've shoved her out the door.

Gen couldn't take her eyes off Remy as he walked in. She wanted to inspect every inch of his body to make sure he was okay. Remy stared at her, never taking his eyes off hers.

"Thank you, Bertha, for watching over my woman. Bailey's van is parked behind the house. Did you get her keys?"

Bertha pulled her hand from her pocket. "Right here. I'll bring it up to the lot."

Bertha stood and walked to the front door but stopped next to Remy. "You're welcome. I'm sure it was quite an enlightening night for Gen." Bertha cackled as she walked out the door, shutting it behind her.

Gen took one step closer to Remy. "I was worried about you. Are you okay? You smell like smoke." She wanted to run to him and search every inch of his skin to make sure there was nothing hidden, but she had to know what happened.

"I'm fine, my mate." He encircled her with his arms and nuzzled into her, letting out a big sigh.

She rubbed his bare back. "Want to tell me what happened?"

He squeezed her tighter. "I lost a close friend."

Gen bit her lip, not wanting to ask a question she needed to. "Is it my fault he snapped? Did our coming here push him too far?"

Remy leaned back, looking into her eyes. "No, baby. I'd lost Jensen a while ago. I just didn't know it until now. He took Megan as his mate."

She thought back to her lesson on when a mate died. She nodded, understanding everything perfectly now. Taking his hand, she led him to the sofa where he pulled her onto his lap.

He ran his fingers through his hair. "Guess in my short time as alpha, I haven't done a very good job reading my lions."

"I wouldn't say that," she replied. Gen had learned a lot since Nana Leandros arrived. "It takes a team to put on a show. Sorta like it takes a team to run a pride. Everybody has a part to play and they practice to become the best they can at their role. If one person is missing, the show must go on, but not as efficiently.

"Your pride was missing a key player, so things got through the cracks. But that position has been cast, and she will do her damnedest

186

every day to be better than the day before to provide love, protection, and support to the pride...and its alpha."

She leaned in and kissed him. It started as a kiss of love and comfort, quickly turning into one of passion and desire. Her body lit up like a tree hit by lightning.

"I'm eager to take you upstairs and try out some of the techniques I'm sure Bertha told you about."

Gen shook her head at Remy. "Please don't ever remind me about that conversation again. But good news, I know all about the mate bite. So, when are you going to give me one?"

Remy's eye glowed golden and he growled, "Right now, love. Let's go upstairs." Remy grabbed her hand and pulled her up behind him. She wasn't complaining; she wanted him desperately. Her heart filled to near bursting with love for him.

As soon as they walked in the bedroom, he spun around and she finally gave him the kiss she'd been thinking about since she was dragged away from the house. Their tongues rubbed and danced, igniting the desire she felt deep in her core. He felt hot, smooth, and his hair was silky between her fingers.

He slid his hand down her back, shoved them into the waistband of her pants and grabbed handfuls of her ass, squeezing her flesh.

She moaned, his touch triggering something inside her. Her mind focused on being his now. Tonight.

She pushed him back onto the bed. He was naked after a shift, she figured. Last she saw him, he was fully dressed. His long, hard cock stood proud, waiting for her touch.

His skin was warm, smooth. She curled a hand around his thick shaft and pumped slowly up his length.

"Ah, fuck, Gen."

She grinned at the desperate way he said her name. Like he was hanging on by a thread. "Tell me what you like."

He lifted his head to meet her gaze, his abs contracting with his movements. "I fucking love everything you do, baby. Every goddamned thing."

She lifted her lips in a smile. "Really?"

"Really."

She lowered to run her tongue in a circle over the head of his cock. A rough growl sounded from him.

"Do you like that?" She did another slow lick and swept her tongue down to his balls, taking each into her mouth and sucking lightly. "Or that?"

He growled. "I love it all, but I'll love your lips wrapped around my dick more."

She snorted a laugh and went back up, taking him into her mouth, letting her spit slide down his shaft and using it to lubricate him as she jerked him in her grip.

"Fuuuck!" he groaned. "Your mouth feels like heaven."

Gen took him deeper, letting him slide in and out of her mouth. He twined his fingers in her hair, grasping her curls. His ass came off the blanket as he thrust his cock into her mouth. Her pussy contracted with every groan and sound he made. She loved that he was enjoying what she did.

His pleasure was making her thirsty to have him inside her. Beads of moisture gathered at the tip of his dick. She flicked her tongue over it, tasting him. He was salty, earthy, and her body craved more.

She sucked him deeply again, taking him farther. His groans got louder and deeper. She worked him with her hand, jerking him faster, sucking him tighter. His grip on her hair grew painful and the thrusts he made into her mouth suddenly stopped. He gave a loud roar as he came in her mouth, his seed spilling down her throat. She swallowed quickly, taking every drop of him into herself.

She didn't get a chance to think about his taste. He slipped out of her mouth, and sitting up, jerked her hoodie over her head. Then her pants went. Soon she was straddling his legs again. He sucked one of her breasts into his mouth, the sensation sending fire shooting to her clit.

"Oh god," she mumbled.

He glided his hands all over her as if unable to get enough of her body. He tweaked her other nipple, pinching and pulling, making her squirm. She leaned forward, pressing her breasts into his face. His lips moved over her skin like a hot brand — taking, tasting, owning.

He leaned back, tugging on her hips. She scooted up until her knees were to either side of his head and her pussy was above his mouth. He curled his arms over her legs and pulled her down to his mouth. She held onto his hair, unsure how low she could go without depriving him of air. When his tongue flicked over her folds, she knew she was at the right spot.

He licked at her pussy, rubbing up and down her sex, sucking at her wetness and biting the insides of her thighs.

She cupped her breasts in her hands, caressing her swollen flesh and pinching her nipples. Her arousal grew in strength and need coursed through her veins like a drug seeking its target.

He licked and fondled her pussy with his tongue, drawing circles and lapping at her like he loved her taste. She sensed he did. Tension curled in the pit of her stomach, winding quickly with every lick he gave her. Every groan and each of her moans only pushed her closer to that moment she knew she'd see stars. Her body shook, making her fall forward to grip the blanket.

He nibbled on her clit and sucked hard, making her fly over the edge. He slipped his tongue into her, fucking her in short, hard thrusts. Pressure exploded inside her and a wave of joy took her by such force. She was left breathless and gasping for air. She choked, her pussy grasping at his driving tongue.

"Oh...oh my god!" she finally got out.

He was at her back in a heartbeat, his cock spreading her pussy folds open and gliding in. He felt massive, filling her so completely, she swore there wasn't a millimeter of space left. Then he reared back and drove forward, sending fire racing through her pussy.

She moaned, her body aflame with need.

"Remy," she moaned, pushing back into each of his thrusts.

"You are mine," he said on a hard thrust. "Always mine."

He dropped over her, caging her under him.

"Always," she breathed.

He took her faster, harder. He curled an arm around her waist and pressed her into him. Then he slid that same hand between her legs and pressed at her clit. "Suck my dick with your hot pussy. I want to feel you tighten around me."

She curled her fingers into fists on the

blanket and let herself go. She screamed this time. Loudly. Her pussy clasped tightly around his driving cock. A searing pain hit her shoulder and she realized Remy bit her. The pain/pleasure took her body to new heights. His body tensed, making his movements jerky at the same time she rode the pleasure wave. His thrusts slowed until he stopped completely, his cock pulsing inside her grasping sex.

He filled her with his cum, the pleasure intensifying for her. Her body shuddered as mini orgasms rocked her core. Her pussy continued sucking hard at his cock.

"Sleep, mate. I will always protect you and love you."

Gen sighed and cuddled into his warm body. "I love you, too, mate."

TWENTY-EIGHT

Gerri Wilder snapped awake but didn't move or open her eyes. She listened carefully to see why her animal woke her. The creak in the floorboard in the hallway clued her in. Her bedroom door silently opened. Peeking through a slightly opened eye, she watched a small beam of light dance along the walls, finally landing on her comforter.

Searching for her, the ray shined over her eyelid and was gone. With shifter speed, she slipped from under the covers, over the side, onto the floor. A couple of quiet spit sounds came from where her pillow remained. A handgun with a silencer.

Whoever had broken into her home was deadly serious. She could play along just as well.

A voice floated on the air. "Did you get her?"

"Stop moving the damn flashlight. I don't know since there's no way for me to see her." She heard clothes rustling. "Give it to me, dumbass. Now."

The door opened farther and a boot stepped in. "What the fuck? Where did she go?" Both humans dropped to their knees and the light swept under the bed ruffle. By that time, she had already been back on the bed for a second.

"She's not there," the dumbass whispered. As soon as the light stopped shining from under the material, she rolled back onto the floor.

"No shit, Sherlock. She's hiding" The men climbed to their feet. "Check the other side." Once again, the light skittered around the wall. Gerri scooted under the bed and laid her head on the floor to watch the beam.

"I can't see anything."

The man with the light grumbled and tiptoed around the bed. These two were complete idiots. If they didn't have a gun, she would've exposed them already. She heard a knee hit the floor with a grunt. The light swept under the bed again.

"Where the fuck did she go?"

Gerri had crawled up the twelve-foot wall and perched in the darkest corner, watching the comedy below. The man dropped the flashlight onto the covers and slapped his hands around the mattress.

Really? She had always watched her weight, but nobody was skinny enough to hide under sheets and not make a bump.

"Bailey said she was a shifter. Maybe she shifted."

Well, that name was familiar. She would have a word with Alpha Leandros tomorrow.

The other human turned on his friend. "Into what? A damn spider?" He turned and shined the light around. "Don't be such a dumbass. She's somewhere."

She latched onto the ceiling and quietly made her way behind the dumbass. Both were dumbasses if you asked her. Planting her feet, she stretched down, grabbed both sides of the intruder's head and twisted it halfway around with a tiny snap. He fell to the floor and she drew back up.

The man whipped around. "What the fuck?" The beam of light swooshed around the room. "I'm getting the fuck out of here. Bailey can kill you herself." He stumbled around the bed then looked over his shoulder.

Gerri swung her legs down, palms attached to the ceiling, then dropped right in front of him. He faced forward and gasped, surprised to see her there. She pressed her finger against his forehead. "Goodbye."

He fell limply to the floor and Gerri sighed.

She stepped over him and lifted the phone on the nightstand. When she heard the other side pickup, she said, "I am in need of your services right now. Two humans."

With that, she made her way into the kitchen to brew tea. It would be rude to not have anything to offer to a guest.

The next morning, Gerri pushed a shopping cart down the grocery store aisle. She was in the mood for cookies, and of course, she was out of sugar. She turned the corner and another cart bumped into hers.

The other woman gasped. "Oh, ma'am, I'm so sorry. I wasn't looking where I was going. Please excuse me."

Gerri looked at a petite redhead standing by her cart. "No worries, dear. Are you okay?" She glanced down at her cart to see what she was buying. You could learn a lot about a person based on their shopping habits.

For instance, she was buying a lot of frozen dinners. She could assume she was single. Gerri brought her eyes back up to the young lady and saw tears form in her eyes.

"Oh, did you hurt yourself when we bumped into each other?"

The woman sniffled. "I'm so embarrassed, sorry. I don't mean to cry on you."

Gerri pushed her cart away and wrapped her arm around the young lady's shoulders.

"There's a coffee shop next door. Why don't you come with me and tell me what's bothering you? I have time and I might be able to help."

The End... For Now

ABOUT THE AUTHOR

New York Times and USA Today Bestselling
Author

Hi! I'm Milly Taiden. I love to write sexy stories featuring fun, sassy heroines with curves and growly alpha males with fur. My books are a great way to satisfy your craving for paranormal romance with action, humor, suspense and happily ever afters.

I live in Florida with my hubby, our kids, and our fur babies: Speedy, Stormy and Teddy. I have a serious addiction to chocolate and cake.

I love to meet new readers, so come sign up for my newsletter and check out my

Facebook page. We always have lots of fun stuff going on there.

Find out more about Milly Taiden here:

If you liked this story, you might also enjoy the following by Milly Taiden:

Sassy Mates / Sassy Ever After Series
Scent of a Mate *Book One*
A Mate's Bite *Book Two*
Unexpectedly Mated *Book Three*
A Sassy Wedding *Short 3.7*
The Mate Challenge *Book Four*
Sassy in Diapers *Short 4.3*
Fighting for Her Mate *Book Five*
A Fang in the Sass *Book 6*
Also, check out the **Sassy Ever After World on Amazon**
Or visit http://mtworldspress.com

Nightflame Dragons
Dragons' Jewel *Book One*
Dragons' Savior *Book Two*
Dragons' Bounty *Book Three*
Dragons' Prize *Book Four (coming soon)*

A.L.F.A Series
Elemental Mating *Book One*
Mating Needs *Book Two*
Dangerous Mating *Book Three*
Fearless Mating *Book Four*

Savage Shifters
Savage Bite *Book One*
Savage Kiss *Book Two*

Savage Hunger *Book Three*

Drachen Mates
Bound in Flames *Book One*
Bound in Darkness *Book Two*
Bound in Eternity *Book Three*
Bound in Ashes *Book Four*

Federal Paranormal Unit
Wolf Protector *Federal Paranormal Unit Book One*
Dangerous Protector *Federal Paranormal Unit Book Two*
Unwanted Protector *Federal Paranormal Unit Book Three*
Deadly Protector *Federal Paranormal Unit Book Four*

Sci-Fi Romance – Guardian Warriors
The Alien Warrior's Woman *Book One*
The Alien's Rebel *Book Two*

Paranormal Dating Agency
Twice the Growl *Book One*
Geek Bearing Gifts *Book Two*
The Purrfect Match *Book Three*
Curves 'Em Right *Book Four*
Tall, Dark and Panther *Book Five*
The Alion King *Book Six*
There's Snow Escape *Book Seven*
Scaling Her Dragon *Book Eight*
In the Roar *Book Nine*
Scrooge Me Hard *Short One*
Bearfoot and Pregnant *Book Ten*
All Kitten Aside *Book Eleven*
Oh My Roared *Book Twelve*
Piece of Tail *Book Thirteen*
Kiss My Asteroid *Book Fourteen*
Scrooge Me Again *Short Two*
Born with a Silver Moon *Book Fifteen*
Sun in the Oven *Book Sixteen*
Between Ice and Frost *Book Seventeen*
Scrooge Me Again *Book Eighteen*
Winter Takes All *Book Nineteen*
You're Lion to Me *Book Twenty*
Lion on the Job *Book Twenty*

Also, check out the **Paranormal Dating
Agency World on Amazon
Or visit http://mtworldspress.com**

Raging Falls
Miss Taken *Book One*
Miss Matched *Book Two*
Miss Behaved *Book Three*
Miss Behaved *Book Three*
Miss Mated *Book Four*
Miss Conceived *Book Five (Coming Soon)*

FUR-ocious Lust - Bears
Fur-Bidden *Book One*
Fur-Gotten *Book Two*
Fur-Given Book *Three*

FUR-ocious Lust - Tigers
Stripe-Tease *Book Four*
Stripe-Search *Book Five*
Stripe-Club *Book Six*

Night and Day Ink
Bitten by Night *Book One*
Seduced by Days *Book Two*
Mated by Night *Book Three*

Taken by Night *Book Four*
Dragon Baby *Book Five*

Shifters Undercover
Bearly in Control *Book One*
Fur Fox's Sake *Book Two*

Black Meadow Pack
Sharp Change *Black Meadows Pack Book One*
Caged Heat *Black Meadows Pack Book Two*

Other Works
Wolf Fever
Fate's Wish
Wynter's Captive
Sinfully Naughty Vol. 1
Don't Drink and Hex
Hex Gone Wild
Hex and Kisses
Alpha Owned
Match Made in Hell
Alpha Geek

HOWLS Romances
The Wolf's Royal Baby
The Wolf's Bandit
Goldie and the Bears
Her Fairytale Wolf *Co-Written*
The Wolf's Dream Mate *Co-Written*
Her Winter Wolves *Co-Written*
The Alpha's Chase *Co-Written*

Contemporary Works
Mr. Buff
Stranded Temptation
Lucky Chase
Their Second Chance
Club Duo Boxed Set
A Hero's Pride
A Hero Scarred
A Hero for Sale
Wounded Soldiers Set

**If you enjoyed the book, please consider leaving a review, even if it's only a line or two; it would make all the difference and would be very much appreciated.
Thank you!**

Printed in Great Britain
by Amazon